Ticket to Tomorrow:
A Collection of Chinese Science Fiction and Fantasy

LIU JUE

First published in 2022 by Royal Collins Publishing Group Inc.
Groupe Publication Royal Collins Inc.
BKM Royalcollins Publishers Private Limited

Headquarters: 550-555 boul. René-Lévesque O Montréal (Québec) H2Z1B1 Canada
India office: 805 Hemkunt House, 8th Floor, Rajendra Place, New Delhi 110 008

Original Edition © The World of Chinese Magazine
The Commercial Press

ISBN: 978-1-4878-0863-1

To find out more about our publications, please visit www.royalcollins.com.

CONTENTS

AN WEI 安蔚

An Wei trained as an engineer with a degree in automation from Tongji University, but left the profession to become a writer. Focusing on fantasy, sci-fi, and screenwriting, An's best-known work is *The Gray* (《灰体》, 2015), a steampunk animation series that has gained over two million views on Bilibili, one of China's top video-sharing sites.

LIGHTHOUSE

灯 塔

I sat up in the canoe and saw the moon hanging large in the sky; the light seemed to drip down like drops of water. The sea breeze rushed past and my cold body couldn't help but shiver. I slowly exhaled a heavy breath and rubbed my eyes with the backs of my hands, maybe too hard; tears almost came out. I looked up at the moon, so round in the sky. Beneath it, there was a thin silhouette in the light. That was my destination.

The canoe rested against a simple pier at the lighthouse. I climbed up, and tied the canoe to the post. I stood at the door of the lighthouse and twisted the handle, but it didn't turn, so I pushed gently and it opened. There was a stairway ahead.

"Is anybody there?" I called out.

After a while, a faint voice filtered down to my ears.

"Wait a moment, I'm coming."

I stood there for a while at the base of the stairs, but

didn't see anyone. I then sat on the steps, facing the open door and looking out at the pitch-dark sea. Because the moon was behind me, I could see all the stars in the sky and the horizon where ocean and sky met.

"I'm sorry for making you wait," the woman's voice said again, but much louder.

I turned around and saw her standing behind me. She was as beautiful as her voice.

"Don't worry," I stood up. "Time is something I have."

"So you're...the new lighthouse keeper?"

I nodded, "Maybe, at least that's as much as I know."

"Well, then that's all right," she laughed, "It's like this with every keeper."

"And you? You're the former keeper?"

"No," she said. "I'm the keeper's assistant."

"And what about the last keeper?"

"Well, he's gone, and now you're here."

"Right. That makes sense."

I followed her up the spiral staircase, endlessly round and round. There were no lights or windows, but it wasn't dark. I felt light flowing down from above. Not long after, her voice became distant again, like it sounded when she first answered me. It was a strange feeling, like the stairs were winding a straight plane round and round the tower. I looked up and found my view unobstructed; I could see the wavering light emanating from the top floor of the lighthouse, just as if I were outside the tower. I couldn't make up my mind whether I was spiralling up or if the staircase was straight. For the first time, I discovered it was easier to lose oneself on a straight road than on a curved one.

I didn't feel lost, though. What kept me alert was the scent of her body. It wasn't just fragrant; it also had a calming gentleness. Smelling her scent, being around her, everything else became unimportant, even spontaneous.

Stepping through time, fragrance, light, and stairs, we came closer to that entrance. When the light almost covered us, she opened a door to the right, and we walked in. After we closed the window, the light was outside. Even though the room didn't have a light of its own, it had a large window. Light from the huge moon spilled in from outside, but it was no longer grandiose, just gentle and calm.

The light in the center of the room illuminated a small wooden table with a wooden chair next to it. In the darkness on the side of the room, there was a single bed and a bookshelf. There were no other furnishings.

"This is your room. If you need anything, you can go to the room upstairs to get me." She pointed to the door behind her.

"So what's my job?"

"To guard this tower." She laughed, "Guard the light; don't let it go out."

I nodded—that's right, that was a keeper's basic job.

I walked over to the bookshelf. There was the keeper's diary and some CDs.

"So many CDs, but no CD player," I said.

"You don't need a CD player."

"I can listen to the CDs without one?"

"I don't know. But the previous keeper never needed a CD player."

"All right, thanks."

"You've had a long journey; you should rest. I'll leave you alone." As the woman finished speaking, she pulled the door open and walked out. The light outside faded.

I toppled onto the bed and stretched. I fell asleep quickly. Naturally, I had no dreams.

I woke up and had a sudden desire to take one of the CDs and put it on the desk with the reflective side up. When the moonlight hit the CD, a sparkling light was reflected, and a solid image appeared in the room. There was a majestic mountain covered in ancient trees. A waterfall flowed down the mountain's face, and small streams joined in and split up again, giving the mountain spirit and life.

In the midst of this vivid imagery, my senses of hearing, smell, and touch were all engaged. It was as if I was there. My mind swirled, and I felt dazzled and intoxicated.

She gently pushed open the door, with my breakfast in her hands. I covered the CD with my hand and put it back in the case, which I placed on the bookshelf.

Breakfast consisted of baked fish, a fried tomato, two slices of bread, and milk. The flavor was bland, and I couldn't tell which animal the milk came from. I asked why she didn't eat with me, and she said it had always been that way.

After breakfast, I sat under the moonlight and read the keeper's diary. The moonlight was neither strong nor dim, and my eyes felt comfortable. I read some time before drifting off to sleep. When I woke up, she had already brought lunch. I closed the diary and placed it back on the bookshelf. Thinking back, I couldn't remember what I had read. It was no matter; there was always time to read it again.

Lunch was fried eggs, an onion salad, two slices of bread, and milk. The eggs were big, but I couldn't tell which bird they came from. The portion was about the same as breakfast. In fact, there was no real distinction in the lighthouse between day and night. The moon had been replaced by the sun. It seemed trivial to insist on differentiating between breakfast and lunch.

She still didn't eat. She just sat on the bed with her chin in her hands, looking at me.

After I finished, she spoke.

"Do you know what a bubble is?"

"Of course I do."

"Not the normal kind, the ones I am talking about are

huge. The sea out there has this type of bubble in it. When they appear, a fish storm is coming."

"A fish storm? What's that?"

"Oh, you'll see when it comes. I can't even begin to explain it."

Hearing her describe it in this way, I didn't want to ask more.

Time went by like this slowly, segmented by meals. In between, I alternated between reading the diary and watching CDs. The keeper's diary gave me a kind of hazy feeling; it was hard to understand what it was about, and I couldn't seem to remember what I'd read afterwards. It mentioned something about the fish storm, but I didn't understand what it was. However, each scene in the CDs was engraved in my memory—whether they were mountains, deserts, grasslands, or great rivers, they were all quite real to me. It was almost as if they came from my own mind. Each time I'd suddenly wake, it was like I had been here many times, and couldn't shake the feeling.

After I don't remember how many days like this, the fish storm came.

On that day, she brought me a rice omelette, asparagus salad, and a cup of milk. She then sat as she always did upon the wooden bed, chin in her hands, staring at me. She spoke:

"In a moment, the fish storm will come."

"Oh?" I said, "Then we have to see it."

"Of course," she said. "It's just that every time after the fish storm comes, some unavoidable things happen, so I don't like it at all."

After she said this, I began to feel the same way, too. It was relaxing and comfortable in the lighthouse, but I knew that the fish storm would upset this calm.

Not long after, there was a feeling of a disturbance in the air and the scent of the sea became stronger. We went to the window and saw the sea had started to toss. After that, the surface of the sea lit up. A number of small bubbles came up in rows, floating into the air. The moon illuminated them in a panoply of colors. A wind blew, carrying the light to a far-off place. The bubbles kept growing in number and size, and some flew past the window—they looked large enough to fit a person inside. They whirled about in the air, and the light danced about, dazzling me; it was exhilarating.

The bubbles suddenly stopped rising from the sea, and the ones floating in the air disappeared far away into sky. The surface of the sea suddenly became calm, giving me a feeling of asphyxiation. Then, the fish storm started.

The surface of the water became dark, and the forms of countless fish were visible, kicking up sea spray all about. Crystalline, transparent fish; fish of all colors; gold and silver fish; giant fish with long wings; small fish like rubies on a thread. Every kind of fish I could imagine—and all the kinds I couldn't even fathom in my dreams—shot out of the sea into the air, churning up huge waves. Soon, there were fish and waves everywhere between the ocean and the sky. It was crazy enough to make you forget to breathe, forget your heartbeat, even forget to think.

As the fish storm ended, I realized I was crying.

I quickly wiped away my tears, so I didn't know if she saw. I knew, though, that she had seen the fish storm many times, so she wouldn't be as moved as I was.

After the fish storm, days went by normally. The only thing that was different was that we were both waiting— waiting for that thing that would interrupt the pace of our lives. We didn't really care about this thing, but we couldn't ignore its existence. It was, after all, a part of the fish storm.

Finally one day, I woke up and knew that it had arrived. I walked over to the window and saw a silhouette approaching the lighthouse. I walked out of my room and down the stairs. Just like the day I'd arrived, I sat on the stairs and looked out over the sea. When the silhouette came a bit closer, she came down the stairs and sat next to me.

"You're different than the previous keepers," she said. "They were never as calm as you."

"What were they like?"

"Like in the diary."

"I've read it, but I don't remember a single word."

"That's natural. What other people have done, heard,

said, seen, and thought—that doesn't concern us. So whether you know or not, remember or not, it doesn't influence our thoughts and lives. Anyway, the previous keepers were different from you, so you can't nor do you need to remember the contents of the diary."

I thought maybe she was right.

"Maybe," I said, "the me of when I arrived could remember the diary's contents."

"Now, you are better suited to be the lighthouse keeper."

I didn't speak aloud the reply that formed in my heart, because it didn't pertain to me anymore.

Later, we saw the silhouette clearly. There was a canoe, and in the canoe, there was a person. When the person came closer to the lighthouse, we saw his face. I saw that this person was me.

I didn't look like I had been when I arrived, natural and carefree. I looked very nervous and hesitant, like I wasn't sure if I should pull my canoe up to the lighthouse. Only when the current had slowly brought the canoe within a dozen or so meters of the lighthouse did I make up my mind and row over, stopping at the base. I jumped out and dragged the boat ashore. I looked back and took a few steps toward the lighthouse. Only then did I see us under the light of the lighthouse.

"I" was astonished; speechless for a while until he stammered: "You... you're here!"

I spoke, "You finally came, too."

"I" sighed, "No matter how different, the same person will eventually come to the same place."

"But different is different." I said, "That's why we split."

"So, in the end, I'll definitely leave," "I" said.

"And I will stay," I said.

"You shouldn't leave," she suddenly spoke to "me." "And right now you can't leave."

"Why not?" "I" asked.

"The dark tide is coming."

"Dark tide?"

"Yes, turn around and look out."

I and "I" looked into the distance, but couldn't make anything out.

"You can't see well from here, but come up to the tower, and then you'll see," she said.

We ascended the tower stairs and entered my room. We looked out into the distance from the window, but could only see a sheet of blackness.

"That blackness is the dark tide, and after some time it will sweep out across the sea and swallow up all the light."

"Just like this lighthouse," "I" mumbled.

"But because the keeper is here, the dark tide has never succeeded in swallowing the light of the lighthouse."

"Will the lighthouse keeper himself glow?" "I" laughed as he looked at me.

"The keeper will keep the light," she said.

"How? That's not a normal tide." I asked.

"Don't let the dark tide enter the tower, and it will be fine."

I thought for a bit and spoke:

"OK, then let's block the door with rocks."

"Wait!" "I" suddenly cried out. "We don't know anything at all about the dark tide, right? And we don't even know why we have to protect this lighthouse."

"Because I am the keeper of this lighthouse," I said. "Of course the keeper must ensure the light is kept."

"I" was speechless for a bit. He wasn't a great speaker— just like me.

We used all the stones we could find to block the door of the lighthouse; "I" had no other choice but to help us. After we were done, I was afraid there would still be a problem blocking out the dark tide. So we built a stone door on the stairs, and then another above it. We built seven in total, for seven segments of the stairs. We used every material we could find—stones, earth, furniture, glass, and all kinds of trash.

After we finished blocking the stairwell next to my room, the dark tide arrived at the base of the tower. We could see its true form.

It wasn't a tide of water.

It was a tide of giant black insects, black beasts, and black-armored knights waving black rifles and giant swords. There was even a black dragon! The dark fiends howled and screamed, spilling over one another. They quickly covered the entire area around the tower. As no light passed through them, we couldn't see them; but we knew they could see us, rendering us afraid, helpless, and desperate. We heard a dull thud from below—they had broken through the first barrier. However, the dark tide didn't lunge forward, but started to circle around the tower. The howling became louder and louder; not just from outside, but also from within the stairwell. We heard another crash—the second barrier was broken.

"It's mealtime; I'm going to go prepare the food," she suddenly said, and then left my room.

"Wait, you're going out on your own?" "I" yelled out, but the door blocked his voice. "I" felt speechless, because there was no way out.

When she came back with the food, the dark tide had already broken through the fourth barrier, but its speed had slowed. We could already clearly hear the buzzing of the insects, the sounds of the individual blows from the beasts, and the clanging of the knights' swords against the stones.

When we ate, "my" hands couldn't stop trembling as he held his spoon. He ate a few bites before giving up, staring at me as I finished my meal.

"I say," "I" couldn't keep quiet any longer. "Don't you think it's really strange? In a huge sea, we don't know where the land is; there's just a lighthouse in the middle of the ocean. Is that normal? Lighthouses are there to guide ships, to guide them to land. Normally, they're built close to the coast, on land or on reefs—but never in the middle of the ocean, because they have no use there! And where does our food come from? Where does the drinking water come from? What's the power source for the light up there; have you never thought about this? What's even stranger is this moon, the fish storm the day before yesterday, and now the dark tide. All of these things are unnatural! Do you remember what happened when we were in the sea before we arrived here? You don't, do you? My memories start from the moment we were floating out on the ocean in that canoe. And now one person has become two people. All of this is just too strange!"

I nodded in acknowledgement that everything "I" said was logical. By this time, the dark tide had broken through the sixth barrier.

We were forced to leave my room and build a final barrier higher up. We used everything we could find, including the desk, bed, and chair from my room.

We finally arrived at the place closest to the beacon.

There was a door, located on the platform on the highest floor. There were no walls up there, just a few slender round columns that rose to the roof. Light leaked out from the door, illuminating the frame around it, shining in all directions. It came closer to us, but didn't seem overly bright. We could almost feel like outside that door was a shimmering world of everything that is beautiful—perhaps more dazzling than light itself.

"The outside world, the real world!" "I" exclaimed.

"That's just another world," I said.

"No matter what it is, isn't this all an opportunity?" "I" replied. "An opportunity to leave here, just when we are about to die?"

"We won't die," she said in a gentle tone, "because the keeper is here."

"I" looked at her and then turned his head to look at me, hope illuminating his eyes.

"We are one person. Without me, or without you, we wouldn't be complete. This sea split us into two. If I leave, we must leave together."

I shook my head. Even though I knew this would hurt "me," I said, "I admit, everything you have said—all of your doubts about this world—are logical. However, I don't need a world where everything is logical and reasonable. I don't need rationality; I just need a world that suits me. It may be wild; it may be ordinary—but I just want to live my life. That door is for you, it's not for me. You and I are different, which is why we split."

He sighed and turned away from us, passing through that door of light. He didn't come back.

There we sat on the edge of the top floor, with our shoulders touching, our backs to the door, our legs hanging outside, taking in the sea breeze and the moonlight upon our bodies. When the moon touched the surface of the water, the dark tide abandoned our lighthouse and fled toward that endless untouchable light of the moon.

"Let's stay together like this," I said to her.

"OK," she said.

Our lives returned to normal, until the next fish storm came. ▪

AUTHOR'S NOTE

This story was written at a point in my life when I felt lost. My job was not ideal, and I hadn't accomplished much in writing. Clueless and directionless, I wanted to give up, to hide, but had nowhere to go. Perhaps the "lighthouse" is that perfect place to hide from reality—and, perhaps, so is writing itself.

CHI HUI 迟卉

Former editor of Science Fiction World magazine (《科幻世界》), a incubator for modern Chinese sci-fi literature, Chi Hui is one of the leading figures of a new generation of sci-fi writers. Many of her earlier works focus on the impact of technology on the spiritual world of people and their environment. Her 2010 novel *Kalemi'an Graveyard* (《卡勒米安墓场》) centered on a young woman, the daughter of a space pirate captain, and her quest to find a mysterious graveyard only mentioned in legend.

THE COLD

冷

I remember that winter. Thick snow weighed on the window's eaves and hung down, stuck on the edge like a quilt roll. My uncle kicked out the door. Shouting family members lifted my dad onto the plank and rushed him to the hospital. I squatted in the doorway, tapping his frozen boots. His toes dropped out one at a time, and I cradled them in the padded breast of my jacket. I thought they could be reattached. I thought doctors had superpowers.

Once I grew up, I learned that doctors did have powers, and that it took a lot of money to become one. My widowed mother didn't have that kind of cash, so I signed up for nursing school. My teachers liked me. Male orderlies were rare and I was a guy, with muscle.

Do you have any idea how hard it is to roll a ninety-kilo patient covered in bedsores? Flesh pours over your hands like a liquid. You can't find a place to grab the skin. Two orderlies need to half-squat in a fighter's horse stance. You both lift from beneath; brace, one, two, three; and flip the patient over.

Later, we were drafted to a field hospital. That was easier. The guys that lay on those beds were scrawny. Sometimes fatter ones were brought into special care, but we weren't on that shift. The floor at our entrance was covered with guts, blood, and amputated limbs. We would roll patients out of the odors of the makeshift ER, and in less than a few days we probably rolled them into the stench of the morgue.

I met a nurse. She wasn't that beautiful, but she laughed with white teeth. Her voice was also pretty. We agreed to get married after the war, but not even a month passed and she was transferred to Wangsa. The city was H-bombed three days later.

The war ended, but it was just another assignment. A few orderlies and I were transferred to the south. It got hotter as we travelled, then cooler. We rode on trains, then boarded an airplane and flew until we reached the South Pole. The sky was a terrifying blue and the ground wasn't white; it was black. It had been bombed. They issued heavy clothing, saying we had to wear it or we would die. There was radiation, that much I knew.

The field hospital was erected rapidly. Even though the fighting was clearly over, it was still built in that rushed army way. The people brought in, however—they were uncanny. Six digits, two heads, four legs, and one arm.

And the arm grew out of their butts. I knew they were aliens, the kind we were fighting. They were frozen solid. Just like my dad when he died.

The doctors were experts. They put together a lot of complicated machines and tubes, saying they could "defrost these fellas."

I hated those "fellas." Thoroughly. They started the war. They dropped the bomb that killed my future wife. But I did my job. If the doctors asked for something, they got it.

There were six aliens in total, and each of them was put in a thawing chamber. The doctors paced the temperatures. They looked nervous and worked cautiously.

A red light started flashing. It was blinding. Alarms went off. The blue observation cells exploded, discharging foul water. It was rancid.

The aliens were all dead. I helped the doctors tidy up and scrub the floor with a brush. We soaked up the rancid water with rags that were wrung out into beakers. The doctors said they would continue their research.

Let them have at it.

I returned to the mainland, resigned from my post, and found a job at a county hospital. I married a widow. She has a nice boy who calls me dad.

Sometimes I dream about that night when I was a child. My dad dug life forms, with four legs and two heads, out of the snow. They were frozen solid. He was hoping to sell them, but it was an unusually cold night, deathly freezing, the coldest out of all the winters I can remember.

The organisms came to life. They touched my dad. He fell. His head cracked open and his toes stayed in his boots. He was frozen solid.

There might be a kind of organism that comes to life in the cold and hardens in heat. But I didn't tell those doctors.

I will always remember that day. I remember crying as I raced over the snow. The strange life forms had left and I thought the hospital could save my dad. His toes were melting in the breast of my jacket. Bloody water soaked through the cotton pads. It leaked into my undershirt and ran down my chest. ■

FLIGHT

飞　翔

0

Any act of flight, departure from the ground, unanchored manner of lift, or propulsion solely by pneumatic or rocket force is unlawful behavior.

- · All parties found guilty of an act of flight will be executed; in addition, three human citizens will be selected at random, deemed guilty by arbitrary association, and executed.
- · Selection precedence will be given to parties acquainted with the party guilty of unlawful behavior.
- · Citizens holding immunity cards will be absolved of arbitrary selection, valid for one round of selection.
- · Reported acts of flight, which result in the verification of the accused party as having engaged in unlawful behavior, are requitable by one immunity card, valid for one person, one round of selection.

—Declaration, Law of Flight

1

This was the last stop.

Lifting her pack, the girl stepped off the train. A box of instant noodles rattled in the small backpack. She was a little nervous, but also excited. If she were found out it would be fatal, and three innocent people would die as well. She stopped there, hesitated, and strode on.

It was a small town. She could easily see to the end of the main strip. Quietly, she asked a stranger cooling himself in the shade about a man who had moved there about two years earlier.

No, no, he hadn't come here to marry. He came by himself. Yes, he probably lives alone. No, maybe not in the actual town, but he would have started out there. Thanks anyways, I'd better ask someone else...Yes, a man, over thirty, he lives alone...

The conversations meandered like that until she finally got a likely address. But it was far—a half-day's walk.

A ride? There were no rides out there. You could take a pedicab part of the way but had to walk the rest. The man lives in a valley, where he started a mushroom farm.

She managed to get clear directions and set off. The autumn air was dry and cool. Clouds of tawny dust rose from the dirt road. Her left foot trod inside the tire rut and her dark jeans were stained with yellow earth.

"This is far," she thought.

But an exiled leader of the old resistance should be living in a remote location, shouldn't he? A smile crept over her face. She'd been searching for a long time. Young people, like her friends, always told stories about him: The only person to fly and live after the strange aliens conquered, fighting for free skies, leading a massive uprising, defeated and going into hiding...Would he ever take the youth flying again? They had wondered.

Her friends took the story for myth, but not her. She had discovered his whereabouts.

The girl's legs were tired, so she sat on the ground and sipped from her flask, watching the road. It stretched into a cluster of lush mountains where the trees were already starting to turn gold and red. The view was beautiful and she felt sorry that her friends would never have the chance to come see it.

It was just talk. Let's go flying or whatever. Nobody thought the boys would actually build a glider. Then somebody reported it. She wasn't involved, so avoided the catastrophe. A laser beam shot down from the sky and struck the boys. Their guts spilled from their bodies. It was horrible.

The boys' acquaintances then waited in terror to see which three would be selected. She wasn't chosen, but her little sister was.

The girl never saw her sister's death. As soon as she heard

the news, she started her journey. Anger burned inside her. She had no fixed partner or companion. All she had to cling on to now was a myth and vague hope.

She put the cap back on her flask, stood, and marched on.

Let me find you, mythical resister, and tell me how to struggle against all of this. Tell me how to fight this unnamed power in the sky.

2

She arrived in the valley at sunset.

A small, spotless white building was spewing smoke from its chimney, while in the doorway a man chopped wood with an axe. He was wearing a T-shirt and gray sweatpants. A tight pattern of sweat beads had formed on his forehead and muscles swiveled under his tanned skin. His jet black eyes looked cold and stayed focused on the swinging axe, which split log after log after log...

The girl hesitated.

"Mr. Qin," she called softly.

The man paused and looked up at the unexpected visitor.

"Excuse me," she summoned her courage. "Excuse me, are you Mr. Qin Yiheng?"

"That's me." He wiped his brow with indifference. "What do you want?"

She waited for a while then said softly, "I want to fly, sir."

He grimaced mockingly, "No, you don't just want to fly, you want fly and continue living, like me. After standing up to those sons of bitches," he pointed to the sky. "You want to continue living, like me."

The girl froze. This was not the conversation she had expected to have with him.

"Let me tell you why I'm here, little girl." He walked over and stood in her face. She wanted to run, but her feet stayed planted.

"Listen," his voice was deep, pulling her in like a whirlpool. "They captured many of us, myself included. But there were still others. They said if I told them where the others were, they would let me go. That's why I'm here, still alive. I'm a traitor. I betrayed the resistance. I betrayed the men, the women, and the children; every single person who believed in me." He bared his teeth. "Does that answer your question, little girl?"

She didn't know what to answer, and he didn't seem to need one.

That night, she stayed in the farm's guestroom. The man didn't have a wife, but he hired an old woman to take care of the farm and other business for him. The girl shared a bed with the woman, with her unwashed teeth and garlic breath, and tossed and turned all night.

The next morning she left without saying goodbye, swearing she would never return to that place.

3

The girl returned to the city and married a man who worked for a small company. Sometimes they took the train or drove a car on holiday. Life went on and flying wasn't an issue, except when they remembered, complaining, about how convenient air travel had been. Later, they had a child and after that the courier came.

It came from the sky lords.

"Due to the recent uprising in America, 122 citizens have been found guilty by arbitrary association. I am here to regretfully inform that you have been selected." It said mechanically. This type of robot was used specifically to notify selected citizens. The sky lords weren't that unreasonable. They gave you at least an hour to make the necessary accommodations.

Her husband turned deathly pale, and the child, who was too young to understand, drew into the father's chest crying. The girl felt like she had been pulled out of her own body.

She had an hour.

"Wait!" She thought of something. It was trivial, but a chance. She grabbed the messenger's cold mechanical arm, as though it were a stick that could save her from drowning, "If I report a crime, can I live?"

The messenger stopped. It seemed to be communicating with its masters.

"If unlawful behavior is verified, your execution will be pardoned," it replied.

"I want to report," she shouted, "Report a man. He has an airplane in his house! He lives in the valley outside the town of Bailin, there's a mushroom farm..."

She didn't know if he really had an airplane. It wasn't likely, but it needed investigating and the longer the investigation took the longer she could live. Live longer...she could at least live a little while longer.

The messenger returned in less than an hour.

Her heart sank.

"The unlawful act you reported has been verified," the robot's voice was still flat. "The criminal has been executed. You have been requited and have spent your immunity allowance. Goodbye, madam."

She stood there staring at nothing. She didn't want to accept that he was dead and that she was left alive.

A voice in her head kept repeating one question: He really had an airplane?

4

She returned to that place in the end.

Her husband had begged and her child cried, but her curiousity was too strong, and once again she walked through the tawny clouds of dust into the now deserted valley.

A month had passed since the mythical man's death. His house was covered in dust and long blades of grass arched over the flagstones. The thriving, verdant color hurt her eyes.

In the backyard she found a stairway. Following the steps all the way up to the mountaintop, she saw a wide, flat piece of turf. Somebody must have leveled it. An airplane was parked in a crude shed at the far end of the lawn.

She walked over, felt the rough wings and handmade propeller. The glider looked like it was made with great care, and it was well looked after.

For a second, she felt the man was standing next to her.

They were both traitors, both resisters, both dead. What did he think about when he stood there: the people he had betrayed? The people who were selected because of him?

He must have been standing right about here.

She imagined the man's gaze and followed it along a ridge that protruded into the vast mountain range. It was a smooth runway that dropped off into a deep valley. Falling from it, the wind would lift you up, and you would soar. ■

FLAME STORM

火焰风暴

They exited the ship shoulder to shoulder. One turned left, the other turned right, and each selected a viewing train going in a different direction.

"Your ticket, Mr. J. Lira."

"Your ticket, Ms. Lumei."

Before hopping onto the trains they looked back and their eyes met. Leftover anger poised itself in their gazes like burning red daggers. They broke the stare stiffly, turned their heads and disappeared into the lines of tourists, acting as if the other no longer existed.

It was not like that at the beginning.

Then came the trivialities, the differences, more differences, and petty conflicts. There were also the hard times they had endured, shoulder-to-shoulder, accumulating grief. It was only after they made the serious step to spend their lives together that they discovered their personalities were like porcupines. If they got too close, they pricked one another.

Neither of them desired sightseeing on Galapade. It had happened after an argument. They both overheated and booked a tour at random. The idea was to take some time apart and find calm. But they were not actually apart.

They were on the same planet.

The viewing train started. The brown-haired man sighed and sat by a window. This line only offered window seats. The wide panes were to give tourists full views on the icy world of Galapade. Temperatures outside the glass were 230 degrees below zero. But inside, it was as warm as spring. The ride was safe and pleasant.

Pumping music started blaring in the car. Irritated, he made a waving gesture and turned on the sound barrier. The surroundings fell silent. That was better, he thought, while looking out the window. It was a cold and quiet planet to begin with.

The dark sky reached deep into space. A light red halo formation ornamented the dim galaxy. It was a cluster of interstellar gas that was lit by increasingly powerful cosmic rays. Below, the flat surface of the planet was shrouded in the glowing haze, while lamplight shining from the view train illuminated crystalline sculptures.

The sculptures were not manmade, but had accumulated over millennia. Oxygen, carbon and nitrogen crystals, even the frozen air itself, mixed in the deep cold and formed octahedral gems with corrugated edges. The gems clustered into sky-high piles with shooting apexes. Not all the sculptures were big and most were in the shape of a steeple. The crystalline clusters went up in stacks and fanned out on the spires like peacock tails. The pinnacles were a light gold that lowered into a light green, which descended into a dark blue, which sank into a murky black. Some of the larger sculptures formed in batches, with the smaller ones sprawling out along both sides, exactly like wings spreading from a bird.

One and two and three, four, and five and six and seven, eight...

The brown-haired man turned away from the glass and rubbed his tired eyes. The first batch had been breathtaking, the second praiseworthy, but this "incredible scenery" was all there was to see along the track. It grew dull.

Like their relationship, at first the feeling was breathtaking, and then it became wearisome. It was hard to believe, but all of the hurdles only added up to a period of ten years. He still loved her. But life had ground those feelings into biting thorns. Just like the refracted glare of the sculptures now stinging his eyes. The train sped along. He called for an attendant, ordered a meal, and started to eat.

The black-haired girl was not sitting in a window seat. She had paid an extra fee to ride in the observation car at the rear of the train. Bunks were provided to lie on and an attendant pointed her to one that looked out of a skylight.

She said thanks and lay down contently. Sliding her hands behind her head, she saw the formation of red gas in the sky and the blue murk around the dead star.

A tour pamphlet she had read outlined the history of Galapade over the course of hundreds of millennia. It was once a fertile planet, but the galaxy's sun had burned at a high intensity and collapsed. It contracted, compressed and exploded, expelling its remains until all that was left was a dense nucleus surrounded by gaseous debris.

Galapade was the furthest of its sisters from the sun and was able to survive. Over time, the planet attracted remnant clouds of stellar gas, which drifted onto its surface. The gases accumulated slowly and formed crystals that were now part of the dazzling sculptures.

People had discovered the planet six years ago. They opened a tour, but were unlucky. The dead star was sweeping up its remnants, causing it to erupt every hundred millennia. Apparently, the next explosion would be soon.

The halo of interstellar cloud was clear evidence: it only turned red when the dead star's temperatures were rising. This gave Galapade wilder and even more striking scenery. But it also put the planet in grave danger.

Danger...Is it dangerous to vacation on a planet with a degenerate sun? Is the probability of reignited nuclear fusion higher than a failed relationship?

She laughed softly, mostly at herself, and rolled over

to sleep, but looking through the skylight she saw cracks forming in the dim, blue ball of gas. They split open and emitted dark red rays.

Alarms rang.

Tourists ran up and down the aisles shouting in dialects. The view train reversed direction, shooting backwards. Lamplight swept over the sculptures, flashing and fading. Seen at a high speed, the distorted landscape had an eerie beauty.

He sat by the window, unnaturally calm among the confusion. At this point even a lonely hero from the movies would be defenseless; a dead star was about to erupt into a sun. Either everyone escapes, or their ashes scatter in the rays. Panic was pointless, he told himself. His fate now belonged to destiny, a driver, this speeding view train, and a spaceship that was preparing to launch.

In an instant, his life became insignificant. He suddenly felt regret. Maybe they should have taken the same train. Then at least he could be next to her.

The train docked at the spaceport. She squeezed out through shouting crowds, stood on her tiptoes and searched for that familiar face. The ship was ready to launch, but she couldn't find him or his train.

Maybe he was already on the ship. A demon began murmuring in her thoughts. In that case, her decision was easy. If he had abandoned her, then she had nothing left to live for and might as well stay behind. If his train was still out there, then she had a reason to wait.

How many people get the chance to burn into ash with a star?

She laughed.

The last view train pulled into the port. He pushed himself first out the door and ran to her.

They stood shoulder to shoulder, looking out of a side porthole as the vessel lifted off. A fire from hell flared up on the ground below.

Rays flashed and the dead star exploded into a blazing sun. A flame storm erupted on the light side of Galapade and expanded, wrapping around the dark reaches of the planet. Flames collided, surged into the sky and diffused into long tails of cloud.

It took an hour for the planet to be fully submerged in the sea of flames. But it almost felt short, only a minute, and at the same time seemed long, as if a whole lifetime had passed.

In the flames below, there were life forms gliding upwards. Wings, coated with glittering crystals flapped above the raging flames. Tails of clustered gems spread gracefully in the fire's glow. The tapered necks and heads were dark black. They looked like birds, but without eyes, chasing the bright red and orange crests, soaring calmly.

The sculptures were living. Sunrays had defused the

stone and crystal charm, freeing the spirits from their cold prisons. One hundred million years of evolution, soaring in one breath.

She put her hand in his palm. It was wide and warm. She felt safe.

"If they could see that moment," she said softly, "I would love to know, when flames encircled them in the sky, what that looked like in their eyes." ■

AUTHOR'S NOTE

These three stories are about anger, freedom, and love. But the most important thing I want you, my readers, to take from them is the simple joy of reading.

FEI DAO 飞氘

Fei Dao is the pen name of Jia Liyuan (贾立元). His works include the short story collections *Innocence and What It Fabricates* (《纯真及其所编造的》, 2011) and *The Storytelling Robot* (《讲故事的机器人》, 2012). English translations of his works include "The Butterfly Effect" and "The Demon's Head." His screenplay "A Long Journey to Death" (《去死的漫漫旅途》), adapted from his story of the same name, won the second Young Scriptwriters' Support Program award in 2009. Fei Dao has a Ph.D. in Literature from Tsinghua University, and is currently an associate professor at the university.

WAR OF THE GODS

众神之战

He wore glasses with a silver frame, very refined, and at first sight, I took him for a con artist. Despite that, I decided to take him seriously. Anyone else would have just thought he was crazy.

"Is this place safe?" He was a little nervous.

"As the head of the National Security Bureau, I guarantee our conversation will not be overheard," I assured the stranger.

He nodded, leaned forward, and raised one eyebrow. "Tell me, why did the dinosaurs disappear?"

I stared at him for no less than thirty seconds, and besides the sound of the persistent tick-tock of the wall clock—everything in the room was silent.

His eyes were full of temptation and excitement, with a certain mischief to them; he licked his lips and asked, "Where did the Mayans go?"

I was fully aware of the gravity of the situation. I put on

a serious face and told him: "Go on."

We spent half an hour in that room, full of his nervous narration and the persistent ticking of the wall clock.

Thirty more seconds of silence.

"Let me get this straight," I said, breaking the silence. "On Pluto, there are intelligent beings called "cleaners." They consider themselves to be the supervisors of civilizations in the universe. That is to say, whenever a certain civilization on a certain planet develop to the extent that they become a danger to civilization as a whole—for example, resource exhaustion or environmental pollution—they intervene. Dinosaurs became too prosperous, so the cleaners decided to redesign them into...kangaroos. As for the Mayans, the cleaners changed them into ants...Did I understand all of that correctly?"

"Right." He appeared elated that I was accepting such an absurd story and answering in such a serious manner. Having deemed me worthy, he decided to reveal more: "As far as I know, the pyramids were built by cockroaches; as for the mice, do you know the statues on Easter Island?"

In that moment, I realized he was saying that all of the great wonders of the world were built by the filthy creatures all around us. I had goose pimples, but I suppressed my indignation. Feigning nonchalance, I asked, "So, do you mean to say that it's the humans' turn?"

"That's right." His expression became serious; he wasn't

stringing me along anymore. "Maybe you don't believe it, but it doesn't matter how vast the universe is. The cleaners' spies exist anywhere there is civilization. Earth is no exception. These spies masquerade as common people, they observe human activity, and report back to Pluto frequently for them to evaluate the situation. They believe that human civilization has lost control, that humans can't fix the current crisis by themselves. The situation could bring problems for Pluto. For this reason, it is necessary to intervene personally. Now, on Pluto, the cleaners are arguing without rest; they will vote to decide what they will change humans into."

"They have a democracy on Pluto?" I asked curiously.

"Democracy?" His face flashed with contempt: "Heh, they are just thugs—arrogant, conceited, moody people. They say that the people on Earth hate each other, they kill each other, and human civilization is about to collapse. They have rated Earth as a second-class ecological contamination and decided to exterminate the infestation. Some have suggested reducing humans to gregarious insects similar to ants. They say this would solve the problem of natural resources and would be beneficial to solidarity and friendship among them. Also, it would put human beings on a rung in the food chain that won't threaten the survival of Earth anymore."

I was secretly shocked. "Do they really believe that?"

"It's a pretext," he said, waving his hand dismissively. "Every time they start a raid, there's always some high-minded reason, but, really, they don't care whether the civilization is a problem or not. They change things because they don't like it. This time, it's pure revenge."

I was amazed by his answer: "Revenge? What did the people of Earth ever do to Pluto?"

Smiling, he answered, "Isn't it true that Earth decided a while ago that Pluto should not be considered a planet?"

"Just for that? That was done by a few astronomers on a whim." I was transfixed.

"But that's what the cleaners are like. They're very vain, and they don't take disrespect lightly."

The thought of these extraterrestrials being so narrow-minded gave me pause. I thought for a while before my next question. "So, how did dinosaurs offend these aliens?"

Impatience was written all over his face: "They say it was because of R&B music. Dinosaurs invented it and loved it, but the cleaners hated that lowbrow music. Now look, you don't need to keep asking about all this boring old news. You are facing a catastrophe; I'm on a special trip to inform you. I hope you can rid yourself of your doubts and report all of this to a higher authority as soon as possible."

His seriousness again aroused my curiosity. "So, are you from Pluto?"

He looked clearly embarrassed and the muscles of his

face revealed his annoyance. "Do you really think that I'm crazy?" With that, he jumped off the chair and threw his silver-framed glasses away. For a single moment, he looked massive; gold brilliance oozed from his face. He sang with a soft, calming voice:

"Ignorant humans, I reveal my terrifying visage to you. You no longer respect the gods and have forgotten humility—forgotten the very appearance of the gods. I am a God of Mount Olympus. In days gone, you prostrated yourself in worship of us, gaining protection at our feet. Today, you sacrifice no cattle or sheep. The world is full of the ghosts of the wronged, falsehood, and cruelty. The suffering gods have already been forgotten. As Hermes, who lost all of my companions, I endure alone on this cold, solitary, alien land, waiting for the morning sun to illuminate the dark universe, to have my vengeance."

The song was so beautiful. I was so engulfed in the sound, I took a full minute to collect myself. "So, all the gods of Mount Olympus were redesigned? Why were the cleaners dissatisfied with you?"

Hate of a thousand years boiled in him; Hermes gnashed his teeth and snarled, "They accused us of being impetuous."

I sighed without judging, "Excuse me, Messenger of the Gods, O Great Hermes, are you the last of the gods left?"

The light fell from Hermes' face as his mood calmed;

he picked up the glasses from the floor and put them on, sitting down in front of me. He changed back into the middle-aged man he was before, but it seemed as though fury was rolling in his eyes. "That's right. We were defeated in a war against the cleaners. All of my companions have been humiliated and transformed. I only survived because I went to Pluto before the war, disguised as one of the cleaners." With this, his face took on a pleased, mischievous look. "The cleaners aren't the only ones who can spy. Of all the gods, I was the most cunning, so I was given this grave responsibility. Through the years, step-by-step, I was able to infiltrate their high-level authorities and learned of their top-secret plans and schemes. I have come here personally to pass on the message. Please, have no doubts or hesitations, prepare as soon as possible."

"Prepare for what?" My fascination was intense and upsetting. I wasn't able to hide it anymore. The whole thing was just too exciting.

"Their interstellar transformation device can undo its previous alterations, but it can only be used after a vote. I will create a diversion after they vote to transform humanity and seize the chance to start the machine. After that—" Hermes eyes were filled with splendor and hope, "—all the gods will be back."

"You mean, Zeus, Hera, Apollo, Athena...everyone will be back?" I asked with caution.

"Yes, and you need to prepare a large reception and help us defeat the cleaners. After that, we will enjoy an eternity of prosperity."

Images of the ancient Greeks and the postmodern world unfolded in front of my eyes: bodies covered in olive oil and hands grasping weapons, fighting against aliens in the sky; on the ground, long-range nuclear missiles are ready to fire at Pluto, with mice, flies, and cockroaches crawling everywhere. "Hey, we could revive all of the divine powers if necessary, so they could be our backup. Think about it. If we revive all the gods, East and West, wouldn't that be a magnificent scenario?"

"Still the hesitation?" the great Hermes asked resentfully.

Waking from my own surrealist scenario, I immediately changed the cordial expression on my face to show him my sincerity. "Hmm, you know, these things are very important. Before taking any action, I have to ask a few questions to better understand the situation and make a wise decision."

From then on, I asked about the particulars of the situation on Pluto, and Hermes' undercover operations there. After I was clear on every detail, I asked nervously, "You know, everything you said is essential; have you told anyone else?"

The great Hermes said proudly, "I haven't. This information is too dangerous, I came to Earth to inform high-level authorities."

"Good." I softened my tone; I felt relieved. I stood up and gave the Messenger of the Gods a steaming hot cup of tea. "I'm terribly sorry; I forgot to offer you a drink. For coming such a long way, I want to show you my sincere gratitude as a delegate of Earth. Please, drink up. I'll pass this report on to my boss." Hermes seemed satisfied.

I decided to act right away, pressing a key on the phone to call out: "Mary, please send Smith into the office."

The situation was clear: there were some problems, but the outlook was still optimistic. In a rare moment of ease and trust, I casually asked, "So, what did those horrible catfish on Pluto transform the Gods of Olympus into?"

Hermes, stupefied, said, "How do you not know? Their external form has changed, but they are the most loyal friends a person can have, they stand by you and protect you."

I understood his implication and laughed: gods, with us morning and night. Hermes lowered his head and drank the tea. As he did, I smiled at him, pulled out my tranquilizer gun and shot him.

I ordered files on my desk as Smith entered, pointed at Hermes who was sleeping soundly in the chair and said, "This gentleman is very interesting. He told me some whoppers, and now he's tired, sleeping very soundly. Wait until he wakes up to deal with him. I'm afraid he's spreading some truly absurd rumors. You know, in this world there are always people like that, claiming to be the savior of humanity. Send him to the care facility for people like him."

Smith nodded. I locked up my drawer and took the key with me, putting on my coat and heading outside. "But, in the future if you find people like this again who want to see me, please let them in. I still want to talk with them. Even if they're nuts, one of them might have something useful to say."

I walked out of the office and into the sun. It didn't look like the world was ending. In the street there were people of every shade and description, gentlemen, gangsters, celebrities, politicians and beggars, each with their own false notions and ideas. Nobody cares if Earth is permeated with fatal toxins, if millions suffer from hunger, or if millions of species go extinct. Would they even care if they knew that there is a group of catfish-like aliens on Pluto who want to turn humankind into ant-like insects? Or of the existence of conspiracies and legends from ten thousand years ago—a hundred thousand years ago? What they need now is the warm sunlight that guides their short, gloomy existence. It doesn't matter if we let them die in ignorance.

At home, I was met by my dog, Bread, as he heard me opening the door. He ran up to me, rubbing my knee on his head. I locked the door and sank into the sofa. What an exciting day. I could finally breathe free.

There's a lot of work to do, work that I can do much

better than those barbarians from Mount Olympus. Those impulsive savages can't do anything right. They are disgusting and they deserved their punishment from those catfish aliens on Pluto.

It's not just gods and cleaners who can do the spying. My people also have extraordinary talents. When the time is right, the world will be back in our hands. The kangaroos will rise again. We will defeat our enemies and take back our kingdom from these barbaric, blockheaded humans.

Bread barked at me twice, I smiled and gave him two doggy treats. He chewed happily as I patted his soft ears, humming some soft R&B to myself. ∎

AUTHOR'S NOTE

When I was a high school student, short, witty stories from science fiction magazines brought me so much joy. These short stories rarely concern serious questions, rather they make us laugh and have one or two smart ideas. After they make us laugh, they are forgotten. Nevertheless, if possible, I prefer writing small stories that will make my readers smile. Laughing is good; laughing is healthy.

LIGHTHOUSE
Illustration by Peng Yue (彭月)

HAN ZHILIAO 寒知了

Having published three well-received novels: *A Fraud* (《骗局》, 2008), *Lost in the Tunnel* (《迷失地下铁》, 2013), and *An Evil Sign* (《凶符》, 2013), suspense-thriller writer Han Zhiliao describes himself as a "heavy addict" when it comes to stories. One of the most notable young writers in the genre of supernatural fantasy and detective mysteries, he has garnered fans with his elegant ideas and tasteful style, rather than graphic depictions of violence and supernatural events that sometimes seem to dominate the genre.

RETURN OF THE CORPHID

魔　花

Francis telephoned right when I was in the greenhouse studying a rare species of Amazonian passion hemp. I had discovered this plant in the north of the rainforest a month earlier. It was an extraordinary species that secretes a neurotoxin capable of inducing paralysis and hallucinations.

"What do you want, Francis? I'm busy," I took the call through bluetooth headphones and continued jotting my observations on a pad of paper while we spoke.

"Gary, what's your schedule like? I need you to come over." He sounded nervous.

"What time? Not now. I'm on a date with my latest discovery—Amazonian passion hemp," I chuckled.

"Forget your passion hemp! I've got something that'll stop you dead in your tracks," Francis raised his voice.

I paused for a second. He rarely took that tone. "Alright, alright, but I'm warning you, if I don't stop dead, tonight's round is on you."

"Deal," Francis replied with relief in his voice.

His strange call had distracted me from my work. I turned on the greenhouse's autonomous control system, picked up my car keys and left.

I wasn't bothered by the interruption. In fact, I was growing curious about this thing that would "stop me dead in my tracks."

Francis was an archeologist and taught with Professor Nash at Columbia University. We had been good friends since high school and went to college together. He had studied archeology, and I botany.

His work with Nash took him to far-off places around the globe. We usually spoke via video calls online or by phone. There were rarely opportunities like this to meet in person, especially the last few years.

I followed the highway to Francis's for an hour before arriving in the small town.

He must have heard the sound of my car. Opening the car door I saw him standing on the porch waiting. I walked up the steps and gave him a brusque hug.

"Don't forget our deal!" I threatened, as we walked into the house.

I stepped into the living room and froze.

"What do you think? I told you this would stop you dead in your tracks! Haha, Gary, your eyes! And your mouth, it's so open I could shove a potato in there," Francis teased, slapping me on the shoulders. But I was in no mind to respond. I stared blankly into the center of the living room, my mind spinning with excitement.

There was a purple plant growing straight out of the floor. It was roughly 1.7 meters tall. The stem was as thick as an arm. The leaves were purple and in the shape of pentacles. There was one big, white flower that had four purple-red stamens and four pristine white petals that overlapped. Even though it was blooming magnificently, it was not emitting a scent.

"Is this real?" Holding back an urge to shout in amazement, I walked towards the plant. It was certainly genuine and definitely mysterious.

"Of course it is. You're the botanist, that's why we asked you to come see it," Francis's wife, Alina, smiled and offered me a cup of coffee.

I accepted the coffee with my eyes glued to the plant and sat down in a nearby armchair.

"To tell you the truth, I've never seen a species like this. Can you tell me Francis, how did it grow out of your thousand-dollar floor?" I finally gained control over my excitement and turned to the couple.

"Oh, over ten days ago, wouldn't you say Alina?" Francis furrowed his brow and turned to his wife.

"It's been a month. We were just coming home," Alina corrected her husband.

"Oh, right. It was a month ago. We had just returned from a holiday. I think I mentioned it to you. We went to Switzerland. When we got back, Alina noticed a light green stem growing out of the floorboards.

"Yes, and Francis wanted to pull it out. But I thought there was something rather magical about it, so I left it, waiting to see what it would grow into," Alina said with a laugh.

"Yes, maybe it's a beanstalk that'll shoot right up into the clouds—haha," Francis joked.

"You really don't know what this is?" Alina asked, turning to me.

I laughed awkwardly. I was a well-known botanist, and it wasn't often that I was stumped.

"I could find its species category, but I would have difficulty determining its name. This is certainly a rare breed. Hey Francis, did you think to ask the floor company what type of wood your floorboards are made from?" I knew most plants would die in those conditions, but in special circumstances it was possible for some to come back to life.

"I asked them, but they didn't believe me and insisted on coming to inspect the floor themselves. Of course they had no clue what it was. At least they agreed to give us a new floor free of charge," Francis said and lowered his head to take a sip of coffee.

"Alright, I'll take some photos back and tell you what I

find," I started taking photos with my pocket camera. "What are you going to do with it? Allow it to continue growing?"

"Alina likes it, and it isn't getting in the way. It is also a rare occurrence worth appreciating. We'll wait for it to wilt before getting rid of it. It's already stopped growing," Francis answered.

"That's fine. But I'd prefer it if the two of you didn't spend too much time in its proximity. We still don't know if it's poisonous."

"I wouldn't worry about that. It's been blooming for over a day now without any side effects," Alina said, looking at the flower adoringly.

I snapped more photos, making sure I captured every aspect of the plant, and then we chatted for a while longer. It was dark by the time I was on the highway again.

The whole drive back I couldn't stop thinking about that strange plant. It was making me nervous.

At home I spread prints of the photos out on my desk and started to research. I worked until the early hours of the morning, but found nothing. Was it an undiscovered species? I was doubtful, but a little part of me was starting to get excited.

I spent the next ten days searching, but there was a void of information. So I sent the photos to some specialists in the field. While I waited for their responses, a strange thing happened.

I was preparing material for an international biology conference in Paris and received another call from Francis.

"Gary," he said, sounding panicked, "I need you to come back here, Alina's sick."

I was stunned, "From what? What did the doctor say?"

"There's no clear diagnosis, the doctor's never seen anything like this," Francis paused, "but I think it's the plant."

"Has it changed in any way?"

"Not really, it looks exactly the same. But a few days ago it started to produce a strong scent. I had someone come test the air and they said it wasn't toxic."

"Then how can you be sure this is related to the plant?"

"Because I noticed that the flower turns, and I remembered something important. It's got to be related to the plant. It would be best if you came over to help me work this out," Francis said with a sigh.

"Alright, I'll head over this afternoon," I hung up. It was almost noon, but at least my presentation was nearly ready. I called my assistant, told him I needed to go out for the afternoon and explained what was left to prepare.

I didn't want to keep poor Francis waiting. He and Alina were a devoted couple. Her strange illness must have been upsetting him. Instead of sitting down for lunch, I stopped to pick up a burger for the road.

Just as I drove into their town, Francis called. He gave me the name of a restaurant and asked me to meet him there. He was already waiting at a table.

It wasn't hard to find in that small town. The lunch rush was over and there were only a few customers inside. I saw Francis waving at me from by the window. He had lost a lot of weight in the ten days since I last saw him. His usually meticulously coiffed hair was a mess and he hadn't shaved in days.

"Thanks for coming, Gary," he said, forcing a smile.

"How's Alina? Is she at home or in the hospital?"

"She's at home. She's obsessed with that plant. She won't leave it for a second. There's something very peculiar about it," Francis knitted his eyebrows and laughed bitterly, "I should have uprooted it when I had the chance. If only I had known then..."

"What exactly is wrong with her?"

"I'm not sure. All her organs are functioning normally, but she's losing a lot of weight."

"You told me you thought there was a relationship between the plant and her illness. Can you explain further?" Francis's face darkened and he let out a long sigh.

"Do you remember that expedition I told you I went on a few months ago?"

I thought for a minute and nodded, "You mean the new tomb that was discovered in Egypt."

"Yes, organized by the Egyptians. Professor Nash has done extensive research on mummies and tombs, so he was invited. I had just finished a project and had some spare time, so I tagged along.

"But when we arrived, we were told they had discovered a whole cluster of graves. These were different from tombs found in the Pyramids. These ones were built into a mountain of stone with a circumference of a few hundred meters. Myriad pathways and tunnels had been cut into the rock and crisscrossed like an intricate spider's web. Signposts were installed to keep people from getting lost.

"The leader of the expedition told us that tombs had been discovered in a few places, but because the area was so large, there were sections that needed further investigating. It was possible that more tombs were hiding behind the dark passageways.

"That excited Professor Nash. Discovering a tomb meant gaining access to a lot of primary data that would advance his research.

"The work started quickly. The Egyptians had already marked the previously discovered tombs and put up signs inside the tunnels. I am fascinated by graves built into mountains. But my work consists mainly of analyzing data and desk research. And none of my projects cover the topic either, so I rarely get the opportunity to visit this type of site.

"The organizers put up warning signs to stop people entering certain areas. But I knew Nash would ignore them and wasn't surprised when he came to find me after he finished surveying the newly-opened tombs.

"Packing headlamps, rope, food, water and other gear, we chose an entrance and walked inside. To ensure we could find our way back out, we made marks on the tunnel walls with a fluorescent pen. But still, we got lost.

"The pen broke and we didn't notice in time. Nash was finding clues and we were marking the wall randomly without checking to see if the fluorescent traces appeared. By the time we discovered the pen was broken, we had no idea how far we'd gone.

"Our only choice then was to try to retrace our steps, but how could we be sure we weren't walking deeper into the mountain? After about two hours we still couldn't find a passage with fluorescent marks. We were both on the verge of collapsing. And that's when we stumbled on a tomb.

"It was in excellent condition. As we had no way to get out, Nash started analyzing the tomb's artifacts and I assisted to one side. We must have worked for over ten hours straight. Almost a day passed before we returned to reality. The food and water were running low. Luckily, the air inside was getting renewed.

"Nash managed to stay calm. He looked at his watch and said the team must have noticed we were missing by now. It was only a matter of time before they started searching the entrance we took. Our best option was to make it easy for them to find us.

"He soon had an idea. There was an air current where the passages crossed. If we burned our clothes, the smoke might get the rescue team's attention.

"So we set fire to our clothes and other bits and pieces. Watching smoke trickledown into the winding passageways brought me a feeling of comfort. We burned everything we could, but there was no sign of a rescue party. Nash was starting to get anxious. But just before we completely broke down in fear, I remembered the mummy cloth—that would burn. I didn't mention it. That cloth had such scientific value that I was worried Nash would berate me for even thinking of burning it.

"While I debated if I should say something, he had the same idea. We walked back to the tomb, opened the coffin, lifted out the mummy and dragged it back to the fire. As we pulled it along the ground, a small ornate box fell out. I picked it up and dropped it in my pocket.

"I tried removing the cloth from the corpse, but it had hardened into a single clump. Nash was in such a panic he just set the whole mummy ablaze. It was wrapped from head to toe in all kinds of spices that smoldered and burned into thick clouds of smoke. God knows how long that mummy burned, but by the time the flames reached its feet, someone had found us."

Francis stopped there, picked up a glass of water, and gulped it down.

"What an incredible tale, and you're only telling me now?" I was mesmerized by his story. Even if it had nothing to do with me, I could still imagine how terrified he must have been.

"Professor Nash is well known. If a story like this were to get out...You know, he's the one who keeps food on my table.

"But what does this have to do with that flower?" I was still puzzled.

"Let me finish. We returned from Egypt and Nash went on to study the artifacts we retrieved. There was nothing left for me to do. But when I unpacked my luggage I found the box that had fallen from the mummy. I'd forgotten to tell Nash about it.

Alina found it beautiful. Of course she had no idea it came from an ancient tomb. She opened it and found a few seeds inside. Right away, I told her to close it, telephoned Professor Nash and brought it to him.

I'm now wondering if that plant grew from one of those seeds. Alina had opened the box on the rug in the living room. My guess is that one of them fell out."

"But what does that have to do with Alina's illness?" I continued pressing.

"Haven't you heard of the curse of the pharaohs?" Francis asked rhetorically.

"That stuff isn't for real, is it?"

"You know, there are some things in archeology that just can't be explained by science," Francis sighed.

Seeing the depressed look on his face, all I could do was comfort him. I wanted to go see Alina, but there was a problem at the lab, so I got in my car and drove back.

Two days later, I had dealt with my affairs and was starting to receive replies to the email about the plant. Most said they couldn't help. But an Australian friend provided some interesting information. He once saw an image of the flower at a site in South America. He assumed that it was sacred to a local tribe.

I was about to open an attachment in his email, but the phone rang. It was Francis. Just as I was about to tell him I'd found a clue, he said something that startled me.

"Professor Nash is dead."

"What?" I stiffened.

"Nash planted the seeds from the box in his garden. His whole family is dead. Their symptoms were just like Alina's. They got thinner and thinner until they were nothing but dry corpses like mummies.

"It can't be possible?" This was unbelievable.

"The plant is evil, it absorbs human life. Before he died, Nash had discovered its origins. It's called a Corphid and originates from South America. It's not clear how it arrived in Egypt. Somehow a local tribe got hold of the plant and started growing it widely. But for some reason the tribe vanished. I'm now wondering if it was the tribe that built the tombs Professor Nash and I visited.

It's an extremely strong plant that can grow out of all kinds of substances. It can even take root in pig iron and could easily grow out of a floorboard. But that's not the strangest part. The flower has some way of absorbing a human being's vitality while addicting the victim to its scent. That's why Alina's getting so thin and won't leave the flower's side. It's possible that this plant nearly exterminated that ancient tribe or forced them to relocate."

"If that's true, then why haven't you been affected?"

"One flower can only consume one life. Alina's weaker than me, so the plant chose her."

"Now what? Are you going to exterminate it?"

"I can't. If I were to pull up the flower now, Alina would die with it. I have to wait for it to start wilting. At least we can spend her last hours together," Francis said with a sob.

I didn't know what to say.

"Do you remember when I told you about the curse of the pharaohs? This is the mummy's revenge," Francis hung up.

I put down the phone and opened the attachment. It was a strange picture: a blotched mural of people kneeling around a gigantic flower. They must have been terrified of its power. Who would have guessed that thousands of years later it would return?

Fortunately, one flower consumed one life and then

withered and died. But nobody knew how it spread its seeds. If they propagated by wind, it would surely be a catastrophe...As I pondered the situation, my assistant came in carrying a flowerpot.

Inside was the same plant that had grown in Francis' living room. ■

AUTHOR'S NOTE

My inspiration for this story came from a piece of old news about ancient lotus seeds excavated from a thousand-year-old tomb that sprouted in modern times. A book I was reading at the time happened to be about the curse of the pharaohs. So, I combined the two elements and came up with "Return of the Corphid." I love fiction, especially fantasy with mysterious qualities, and I love creating stories like this. Don't read too deeply into it, because it's just entertaining and fun.

RETURN OF THE CORPHID
Illustration by Yao Yao (姚瑶)

KANG FU 康夫

Kang Fu graduated from Tsinghua University and has studied in Israel. Once a prolific traveler, she now spends most of her time at home as "an unknown screenwriter, idler, author of unprofitable books, and lover of monster legends and food." She has published *The Jobless Journey* (《失业之旅》, 2014) based on her travels, and a novel, *The Gray Cat Curiosities Agency* (《灰猫奇异事务所》, 2017).

HELP WANTED

洗碗工招聘指南

The other day, talking to some people familiar with the food and beverage industry, I heard an amusing story.

There was a Mr. Song who opened a chain of fast food restaurants, mainly catering to white-collar workers. In this business, the earnings are stable, but the barrier to entry isn't high, so competition is fierce. Aside from ingredients, sanitation, and taste, improving the table turnover rate was the real nut to crack. Song hadn't been in the business long, but he was already somewhat well-known in the industry, mainly because of his impressive turnover rate.

"You know, since fast food restaurants are small, we can't afford a large dishwashing machine; plus, it takes too long to do a load. It's not suitable to our turnover rate. You can buy more dishes, but you'd have to find a place to store them, so those of us in the business have to hire dishwashing employees. Still, it's hard to find one who works hard and has the skills."

Song was reclining in a lounge chair at a resort, enjoying an iced coconut and chatting with a Mr. Li. Li was an internet guy and entrepreneur. After doing breakfast burritos, nail salons, takeout, and beef brisket noodles, he'd gone into fresh-squeezed fruit juice. His brand got a lot of hype, but the customer experience left something to be desired. Market research showed that it was because wait times were too long. Li had heard about Song's miraculous turnover rate, and came to seek his advice.

"In order to ensure freshness and cleanliness, we wash the fruit on-site after the customer places the order. One cup of juice requires a bunch of different fruits that must each be washed, cut, and squeezed, which is why it takes so long. Our customers are annoyed, but we can't install an industrial dishwasher in a mall!" Li was fretting.

"So what you need are suitable workers to do the washing," Song paused meaningfully.

Li saw his opening. Coconut in hand, he scooted closer to Song's chair, begging, "Tell me your secret." When Song didn't make a move, he added, "If you tell me, you can name your price; I'll write out a contract and wire you the money right away."

Song's face creased into a smile: "*Ai-ya*, look how serious you are, how could I charge you? We were at Yellow River Business College together! Anything you want to know, I'll be sure to tell."

It turned out that Song had grappled with the same problem for a long time. He'd tried a number of different solutions, such as washing the dishes himself, giving out bonuses, and even training his own team. Nothing worked. The reason was simple: dishwashing wasn't a job with much room for advancement, and most who took it up had just come to the city and needed a springboard to a better job. Nobody was trying to make a career out of this, so nobody took it seriously, nor wanted to be trained. "If only I could find someone who really loves dishwashing," thought Song; but where would someone like that be found?

He tacked up a sign in the window of the restaurant that remained there for a long time: "DISHWASHERS WANTED. ROOM AND BOARD. HIGH SALARY." But the dishwasher of his dreams never showed up.

One day in the fall, Song was going over the accounts in the restaurant. A man of average height and a round face hesitantly entered the store. Song thought he was there to eat, and was about to tell him that the restaurant was closed for the afternoon and would re-open at five, when the round-faced man pointed at the faded sign, and timidly asked: "Are you still hiring?"

Song picked out a rural accent in the man's voice, and figured he hadn't been in the city long.

"What can you do?" Song asked.

"Wash dishes," the man replied.

"Lots of people can wash dishes," Song rejoined.

"I can only wash dishes," said the man.

This got Song's attention. He looked the man over. He wasn't thin or fat, and looked quite nimble and spry. His messy hair and large ears stuck out. His eyes were big and round, with prominent dark circles around them; maybe he was not getting enough sleep? The weather was quite warm, yet the man was dressed in a dull brownish-gray sweater, with a black-and-white striped scarf around his neck.

"You can only wash dishes? What does that mean?" Song scrutinized the potential hire.

"What I mean is, I'm really happy washing dishes; it energizes me. I can do it quickly and do it well; nothing else does it for me like washing dishes."

"For real?" Song was shocked. "There's someone who loves washing dishes?"

"Absolutely!" the man replied earnestly. "When I see dishes in the sink, my hands itch. If I go a day without washing dishes, I feel empty."

"I find that a bit hard to believe. Why don't you try it for a day first?" Song said.

The dinner rush soon started, and Song led the man into the back kitchen. Customers poured in, and a steady stream of bowls flowed back. The new dishwasher's eyes lit up; he rolled up his sleeves, and got to work—hands flying, water splashing. He'd pick up a bowl and washcloth, spin the bowl around, and let soapy foam form a whirlpool in the sink. Soon, a pile of freshly cleaned bowls was assembled to the side. Song and the other employees watched in awe, almost forgetting to prepare the food as the dishwasher deftly whipped his cloth.

More and more customers came, and dishes streamed into the back kitchen. Normally, at this time, the washing station employees would be complaining that they'd never get through this mountain of unwashed bowls, and some bowls might even be broken in the chaos. Under the new dishwasher, though, the bowls almost didn't have enough time to pile up.

When the restaurant closed for the day, Song asked the worker to stay behind.

"Have you worked in a restaurant before?" Song asked.

"No," he said.

"What are you looking for in terms of salary?" Song was running numbers in his head.

"Doesn't matter. Just room and board, and fruit to eat."

Song's heart skipped a beat, and he felt uneasy. Going around, looking for work and a place to crash, not even wanting money—wasn't that just like the fugitives they showed on the news?

"Where are you from? What's your surname?" Song asked cautiously.

"My name is Xiong. I'm from the mountains." It didn't

seem like he was lying.

Song took another look at the man. He wanted to ask for the man's ID, but then, even if the man showed it to him, it was probably fake. Might as well just leave it, he figured.

Thinking it over, he decided to take the man on, and brought him to the workers' dormitory. As they arrived at the bunk, Song saw Xiong open the small backpack he carried. Aside from a change of clothes, it was empty except for a few apples.

"All right, then, you're on; I'll make sure you're paid," said Song.

"Don't forget the fruit, I need those," said Xiong. "I'm vegetarian; I have to have fruit at every meal."

That was a bit of a pain, Song thought, but he didn't bother to reason with the man. He arranged to have some fruit brought in specially for Xiong every day with the supplies.

In the following two months, there were no flaws in Xiong's performance. No matter how many customers came in, the kitchen operated smoothly. Xiong worked with deftness and ease. The table turnover rate skyrocketed, and Song was in great spirits. There was just one small problem: The other staff who bunked with Xiong complained that he was constantly eating fruit whenever he wasn't working; all throughout the night, they could hear him crunching and gnawing, making it impossible to sleep.

Song felt there was no way he'd get rid of Xiong; in fact, if he could find another one like him, he would fire all those other whiners.

Song paused at this point in his story, and took a few big sips from the coconut. Li was completely entranced.

"So was this guy not human or something?" Li asked.

"You guessed it," said Li. "We suspected from the start."

"So then what happened?" Li asked.

"Well, I got more and more curious, but I didn't want to ask directly, so I thought up something—detective work."

Businessmen are a superstitious lot, and all kinds of feng shui "masters" plied their trade in the city. Song was no exception, and had the number of a "Master Wise Eyes" saved in his phone. Bringing along an old and valuable cake of Pu'er tea, he went to the master and briefed him of the situation. "I can take care of this," the master smiled. "I already know what to do. At the start of next month, invite me to your restaurant under the pretext of inspecting the feng shui. When I come to the kitchen, just subtly point the worker out to me and, using my magic mirror, I'll be able to find out what kind of spirit it is."

Song was overjoyed. He required, though, that the master simply tell him what Xiong was, not drive him away. A worker like this was very hard to find. He didn't want to mess with a good thing.

Soon the master came by according to plan, making a

show of doing a feng shui inspection. As the restaurant filled up, he remarked: "Oh, I forgot to inspect the kitchen. Such an important place deserves a good look-over."

The master went into the back kitchen and saw a man with messy hair working hard at the washing station, intent upon his task. As the master crept behind the man, he whipped out a mirror from his robes and pointed it at the dishwasher. Song's heart was beating like a drum. If Xiong's true likeness was revealed, the customers might be terrified; and if the dishwasher was really a spirit, then was he good or evil? Seeing the master's eyes grow wide with shock, Song leaned over to look, his heart pounding, his throat tight—

The creature in the mirror wasn't a ferocious beast, but neither was it the same dishwasher as before. It was furry, round-bodied animal with small limbs, a gray body, and dark circles around its eyes. A black-and-white striped tail grew out of its body. As Song stood there, the master calmly put away his mirror, and continued with the inspection. The two of them quickly exited the room.

"So, what is it?" Song demanded.

The master chuckled. "You haven't seen one before?"

"I think I might have, but I can't think of what it's called."

The master was roaring with laughter: "Something that loves washing, and eats fruit for every meal? Come on, man. A raccoon!"

Song was hit by realization. "A freaking raccoon!"

The master spoke: "That's right. Aside from a raccoon, who else would love washing dishes? See, this is why he's so good at his job."

Song's astonishment turned to joy: "So then there's nothing to worry about? No danger in keeping him around?"

"Relax, these animals are gentle. As long as they have enough food and sleep, there's nothing to worry about. However, you do need to be careful: They hate oath-breakers. If someone promises something and goes back on their word, it would be disastrous."

At this point, Song paused his story again, looked at Li, who was deep in awe, then continued.

That day after the master left, Song was in great spirits. He bought a basket of fruit and went to talk with Xiong. Actually, he just asked a single question: "Mr. Xiong, I see that you're quite good at this job. I guess everyone from your hometown is. Could you find some friends from home to come work here?"

Xiong agreed, and took a trip home. Soon, he returned with a few village-mates who all looked and sounded like him. Song prepared all kinds of fresh fruit and received the new workers warmly. He didn't ask where they came from. On the second day, he laid off all the other dishwashers and brought in Xiong's people. There were no more complaints from the dormitory. They all lived together; they ate fruit whenever they wanted.

After this, the efficiency of the kitchen skyrocketed, and the business became better and better. Song saved up money to expand, and soon investors were coming by, wanting to finance a chain. That was all thanks to his efficient raccoon staff. People couldn't figure out how his restaurants could have such quick table turnover and low labor costs.

Li looked at Song with admiration as he finished his story. "I had to put so much effort into convincing my backers, whereas you didn't have to do anything; they came knocking on your door!"

"I don't have superpowers," said Song. "Raccoons are auspicious animals; gods of wealth. They brought all the good luck to my restaurants."

Li was totally converted.

"Now, it's only because we were classmates that I've told you my secret," Song reminded him, tapping the now-empty coconut.

Li nodded. "I know, I know, I won't tell anyone." He hesitated for a second before changing his tone to ask Song. "You know, if I could also hire some of these raccoons to wash fruit, I wouldn't have to worry about annoyed customers anymore. Song, could you, uh, have your raccoons introduce some employees to me?"

Song looked at him with an enigmatic smile, and Li added quickly and apologetically: "Song, please don't misunderstand, I won't steal your employees. I'm just saying, raccoons might also suffer from unemployment problems, so if we provide good jobs and good salaries, we can lift them out of poverty, and we'd be doing a good thing..."

Song waved his hand, cutting him off. "You're overthinking it. I'm willing to help you. However, it would help if you could do the raccoons a little favor."

"What is it? Tell me!" Li beat his chest with confidence.

"Well, you make fresh fruit juice, so you have your own supplier, right? I hear that it's all imported, and organic?"

"Of course, we have a great supplier who brings in new stock every day. It's all Grade-A stuff. It's hard to find on the market here, even if you have the money to pay for it!" Li declared proudly.

"Great. OK, well I have so many raccoons at my place, and they just burn through fruit like crazy every day. I do fast food, I don't understand fruit, and I don't have a suitable supplier. Can you go to your supplier and order a year's supply of fruit? Pay in advance, and have them deliver it every day to us. The money for the fruit you can consider my headhunting fee."

Li was a bit taken aback; he hadn't expected this kind of request. The cost for a year's supply of fruit wasn't small, although compared with his urgent needs, it wasn't much. It was the investors' money after all. Plus, if he didn't improve the quality of his customers' experience, the investors might back out. Thinking it over, he saw what was his priorities were, and said firmly, "No problem. It's done."

Song kept his word. When he saw the invoice from the fruit company and got the first delivery, he immediately sent a few dishwashers over to Li—no, fruit-washers. These new employees were featured in Li's new advertising campaign: "Freshly washed and squeezed, cleanliness you can see."

As night fell and business slowed down, Song closed his restaurant. A group of raccoons gathered around the table, waiting for Song to bring the fruit. Their eyes were round with hunger.

"This imported fruit is great!" The raccoons held the fruit in both paws, burying their faces in it, letting out sounds of joy.

"I didn't think Boss Song's trick would work. Humans are really easy to fool," said one. "Still, won't they soon find out that we can't wash fruit?"

Thinking of the plump fruits rolling about in their stubby claws, the raccoons all guffawed.

"One of the guys they sent over is Claws Joe, from the same part of the forest as me; his arms are so short he can't even wipe his butt. How's he supposed to go wash fruit?" said another raccoon, making all of them laugh again.

"Who cares after they find out?" Song spoke up. "He's not going to admit to anyone that he hired raccoons. He's already paid for a year of fruit, so we're covered for the year." He no longer looked like the Mr. Song who had shared a lounge chair with Li. He'd taken off his suit and shirt, changed into a dull brownish-gray sweater, and wrapped a black-and-white striped scarf around his neck; all of a sudden, he was a raccoon again, albeit one with an air of authority, with some real raccoon gravitas.

"I gotta ask, Boss, how did you think this up?" one raccoon slurred, his mouth full of apple.

"Ah, just a little trick from business school. Present yourself, dangle profits, wipe away worries, and eighty or ninety percent of people will take the bait," another raccoon answered on Song's behalf. "Humans only think about getting rich. They don't understand that the sweets you tricked someone out of always taste sweeter."

"But what if Li finds out that the guys we sent over can't wash fruit? What if he takes our stuff back?" asked the previous raccoon.

"No way." Song chuckled. "You missed a little trick I threw in when telling my story. I made it clear to Li that the feng shui master said raccoons hate those who break promises, and will be sure to retaliate. I'm sure Li wouldn't take that risk. Relax and enjoy the fruit."

"Speaking of which, what are we going to do after the year's up?" a young raccoon was worried.

The large raccoon next to him swatted his head. "Quit worrying. In a year, we'll just find another way to trick humans."

Just like that, all the raccoons' worries were gone. They lowered their heads and tucked in. The room was soon filled with the delicious fragrance of fruit, and the festive sounds of crunching and slurping rose in the air. ■

GETTING LUCKY

招　财

In the capital, there was a poor merchant surnamed Hu who sold fish at the wet market. One day, he found a stray cat and took it in. The cat was orange-yellow, but its four paws were white—what people called a "snow paw" cat. It would also frequently rub the side of its face with its right paw—thus, Hu named it "Lucky[1]."

Hu rose early and lived frugally; after two or three years, he had enough savings to rent a store. After a few more years of hard work, he finally managed to buy a shop. Unfortunately, the building was condemned, and he wasn't allowed to start a business there. By the time Hu found this out and went after the seller, the man was long gone. Angry and worried, Hu fell sick. Without a source of income, his family subsisted on scraps, but Lucky still had a fresh fish every day, and never suffered.

After a month, Hu's savings were almost depleted, and his case wasn't getting heard. The entire family was panicking.

---

[1] A cat raising its paw is said to "beckoning" wealth in Japanese mythology, which has since been adopted in China

Hearing that the Temple of Great Awakening in the west of the city produced great results, Hu bathed, changed clothes, and went to pray in spite of his poor health. Recalling how his years of hard labor had been wiped out in a moment, leaving his family in dire straits, he couldn't help but start crying in front of the Buddha.

After Hu returned home, nothing much happened. Within a few days, the family was completely broke, without even enough money to buy warm clothes for the winter. Hu let out a long sigh; his sojourn in the capital was over—no choice but to return to the village and farm. Thus, he put together enough money to buy a train ticket, packed his belongings, and prepared to head out the next morning.

That night, Hu tossed and turned, unable to sleep. Suddenly, a young man in yellow robes appeared to him, saying: "Don't be in such a hurry to leave. Things may still take a turn for the better." The man didn't look like an ordinary person, but had a round face with two big, bright eyes. Before Hu could ask for more, he suddenly woke up; there was nobody else in the room.

The next morning, someone from the sub-district office arrived with a document in hand. It said that in this time of peace, prosperity, and the glory of all things, the capital would construct subway lines to facilitate transportation. Hu's building was on the planned route, and scheduled to be demolished. But not to worry, the nation cared for the welfare of the people and would handsomely compensate the owners.

So there was light at the end of the tunnel. Things were, indeed, taking a turn for the better. Thinking about the young man in yellow from his dream, Hu thought he must have been a bodhisattva. Hu quickly returned his ticket, prepared chicken, duck, and fruits, and took his family to the temple to give thanks. They bowed their heads and kowtowed before the Buddha's statue to show gratitude.

After some time, the compensation arrived—it was indeed a windfall. That night, the man in yellow appeared again by Hu's bedside, instructing him, "Now that you've escaped poverty, you should make plans for your wealth. Use the money to buy a store in the city center with good foot traffic. Buy real estate in good school districts, the more the better."

Hu heeded the advice. Not long after, property prices in the city blew up. Shops and residences, whether new or old, beautiful or decrepit, exponentially increased in value. Hu simply rode this wave and, with some smart financial planning, became quite wealthy in a few short years.

Hu was very well aware that this wealth was a gift from the bodhisattva, and his piety increased hand in hand with his prosperity. At the start, he just worshipped at the temple, but gradually he started to give to charity, free captive animals, and, later on, donate generous amounts to build temples and invite Tibetan monks to be his honored guests.

In just a few years, he found himself on the brink of his forties. As a child, a fortune-teller told him that things would "go downhill" when he was forty. Because of this, he was cautious. On the eve of the new year, he promised that he would become an ascetic and cultivate good fortune. The entire family, old and young, driver and nanny, all gave up meat, even refusing to use pork fat for cooking. Lucky was no exception; his daily meals of fish, shrimp, and sashimi became tofu soup mixed with soft rice and buns, which was supposed to mimic the taste of dried fish.

One afternoon, Hu was copying scriptures near the window, lost in thought, when he suddenly saw the man in yellow outside; he quickly stood up and saluted. Seeing the man's hollow cheeks and furrowed brows, Hu was concerned: "I haven't seen you in a while. Why do you look so tired?"

"Your life of luxury peaks here," the man answered. "I came to say goodbye; take care of yourself."

Hu was shocked, and hurried over to the man, seizing him by the arm. "I've been earnest in my devotion to the Buddha. I've not been neglectful. Why would the bodhisattva forsake me so? Even if it's too late, tell me what I did wrong," he pleaded. The man in yellow robes shook his head and sighed, but left without answering.

At this time, Hu woke with a start, and discovered he

had fallen asleep in his chair while copying scriptures. He hurried outside, but there was no sign of the man in yellow. Beneath the parapet, though, he heard voices. It seemed like a few people were chatting, but the voices didn't sound human.

One voice spoke: "The High Minister descended to the mortal realm as a cat, and saved Mr. Hu from poverty as thanks for saving his life—he is truly an exemplar among gods."

Another answered: "Mortal life was bitter, but that wasn't the issue. It's just that this Hu takes whole fish and chunks of meat to the clay statues in the temple, yet treats my true body with tofu and soaked bread. Preposterous! How could he possibly not be aware that cats are the so-called bodhisattva of this world?" It was the voice of the young man in yellow.

A female voice joined in: "Humans have always focused on the trifles without looking at the core; they value appearance, but neglect the substance. In practicing religion by the book, they believe they can accrue merit through good works, but they're just fooling themselves and others." The other voices joined in in agreement.

Hu was shocked to hear these words, and ashamed. He peeked over the wall, and saw five cats under the rafter; in the middle was Lucky. The cat on the left had a black forehead and white face, with the look of a judge about him. To the right was a female calico, which looked like a grand lady. There were also two stocky black cats with bright eyes, which looked like guards.

Lucky enjoined: "The mortal world is foolish and there's no need for us to stay. Let's go back to heaven." The two black cats saluted, dropped down on their forepaws, and pushed back on their hind legs, their hair standing on end. Seeing this, Hu hopped over the wall and practically rolled over to them. He prostrated himself upon the ground and kowtowed repeatedly: "We humans are stupid. I thought the statue was the true deity; I really was foolish. Now that I know that cats are the real gods of all things, I promise to serve faithfully and with dedication. I beg you to please forgive us our ignorant crimes."

Hearing this speech, Lucky strolled toward Hu, and patted his forehead consolingly with a white paw: "Although I've already made up my mind to go, you did save my life, and take care of me for so long. I will not forget."

As he finished speaking, five colorful clouds descended, and the cats stepped aboard with dignity. Hu stayed on the ground, kowtowing as they flew away.

After this, Hu no longer built temples or bowed to bodhisattvas, but fed every stray cat he came across. He placed statues of Lucky all around his house, and, rather than burning incense and presenting flowers, made offerings of chicken, duck, fish, and shrimp. In the years later, even though the property market tanked, Hu's assets always avoided disaster, and the returns stayed plump.

Hu would tell everyone he met: "If you desire wealth, be a slave to cats." People liked the idea, and followed suit. In time, it became a saying known to all. ▪

AUTHOR'S NOTE

I hesitated to write about these raccoons—I didn't want to reveal their secret to the public. My roommate disagreed: "People would be happy to know there were such animals among them. Many people are unhappy about living in a world of humans." Our cat didn't object, either. "Just don't give away too much," it instructed, licking its chops. "If these stories make money, I can get better food to eat."

LI ANGAO 黎安高

Li Angao is an amateur writer who works full-time at a bank. As a teenager, he became a passionate reader of Chinese martial arts, whodunnit, epic-fantasy, and techno-thriller novels. In June 2017, he published his first story, "The Welwitschia Plan" (《千年兰计划》), in Science Fiction World magazine. He earned his BA in Finance from Central South University in China, and has a MSc in Sociology from the University of Edinburgh.

TICKET TO TOMORROW

移居未来

1.1

"Hey! It's moving; it's moving!" Oliver prodded Roland with his elbow.

Roland stood up, only half-awake. They'd been napping in turns, resting their heads on each other's shoulders. It was October in Beijing, and the scent of autumn was strong in the air. Roland took a deep breath; the chilly atmosphere struggled in vain against the weariness of his body, and was finally defeated with a drawn-out yawn.

Oliver took out his phone. It was seven in the morning, and the first rays of the sun were breaking through the curtain of darkness. He turned his stiff neck and remarked: "The early bird gets the worm. The lines are even crazier than the real estate lottery twenty years ago."

Roland grunted absentmindedly in agreement. He pushed up the bridge of his glasses and stood on his tiptoes, looking over the sea of heads moving about the long line extending to the entrance of the Glittering Era VIP Hall. The line wound around the movable barriers within the plaza. Then, like a snake slowly uncoiling after a winter's hibernation, the crowd suddenly started to move, dragging itself into the postmodernist structure.

Oliver and Roland followed. In about five minutes—plus one night camped outside the entrance—the two entered the VIP hall. The interior was vast and bright, the crowd gradually spread out. Just as Roland was wondering which way to turn, an usher guided the two of them to their seats.

The space had been temporarily filled with school desks. Already, the ten rows closest to the stage were full. Oliver and Roland sat side by side; although the desks' writing surfaces weren't very comfortable, at least there was plenty of space, allowing them to stretch their stiff muscles and bones.

The emcee came on stage, speaking with passion in a booming voice: "Respected guests, thank you all very much for attending the fourth lottery for tickets to the Glittering Age! Drawing will commence at eight minutes after eight o'clock! According to the Notice Upon Further Stabilization of the Long-Term Temporal Emigration Market issued by the State Ministry of Temporal Resources Management, with respect to customers' demand, private placement has been made at a fixed price for temporal emigration terms in the order of fifteen, twenty, twenty-five, thirty, and sixty years.

"For the current temporal migration plan, no matter the term, all winners will enjoy the privilege of taking along their spouse and family, for a total of up to eight people for the entire duration of the zero vital-sign cryostasis." The emcee paused meaningfully. "That is to say, these current regulations are extremely suitable for taking your entire family along as temporal emigrants. In this drawing, of the fifteen hundred of you seated here, there will be a hundred VIPs who have a date with the Glittering Age! Run towards the future! Run towards your own Glittering Age!"

One corner of the hall spontaneously burst into applause, and in the following few seconds the clapping spread across the room. The lights shone in the guests' eyes, as if their own enthusiasm was about to spill out of their bodies. Some of the guests had already sat down, but stood up again to clap. "I sincerely hope that you will be among those hundred winners!" The emcee waved his arms, putting on a performance.

Oliver clapped along with everyone else; turning his head, he caught a glimpse of Roland cupping his chin, unmoved by the speech. Oliver pounded on his desk, shouting, "Bro, we are definitely gonna win!"

Roland's heart skipped a beat. He knew that Oliver thought that he wasn't joining in because he was unhappy with the fifteen-to-one odds. In fact, the thought of being frozen for twenty-five years and waking up in an unfamiliar world didn't seem such a wonderful prospect to him as it did to Oliver.

Besides, everybody knew that temporal emigration was a huge bubble. Prices were already ridiculous, and climbed every year, continually breaking records. Still, willingly or not, tons of the rich and middle classes were rushing into it. Roland sighed a little. He was rational, but he couldn't fight off his wife's constant refrain of "let's head toward a better future," so he'd waited in front of the VIP hall since ten o'clock the previous evening.

3.1

The automatic door, wide enough for two, slid upward. The man quickened his steps as he walked into the office building. Sensing that nobody else was coming in, the entrance slid down with a whoosh, sealing the frame tightly against the sandstorm outside.

The man took off his airtight purifier helmet and balled up his sand-covered cloak, stuffing it into his lobby cubby-hole.

"Mr. Li, good morning!" Little Xing, the robot receptionist, greeted him at the front desk, as it did every morning. Little Xing was built in the form of the company's mascot—a doll in the "chibi" style of the previous century, with a spherical head and huge eyes, like an anime character.

A century goes by quickly, and technology progresses,

but that hasn't cured the temporal industry of the bumptious tastes of real-estate firms.

The man raised his eyebrows, not stopping as he walked toward the elevator. "Morning, Xing."

"After meeting today's client, will you be formally retiring?" As the man walked over to the reception desk, Little Xing extended its arms towards him, a small box in its hands. It had the logo of Fuxing Temporal, and beneath it, the words "To Comrade Li Huan."

The man paused for a second, mulling that, although Little Xing had been in service for three years, aside from a "good morning" each day, this was the first conversation they'd had.

"Thank you for your twenty-nine years of service to the company!" Little Xing placed the box into Li's hands. "This is a small gift from us to you."

"Thanks," Li nodded, put on a smile, and walked over to the mag-lift.

Once inside, Li pushed the opening mechanism on the gift box. A small hologram of Fuxing Temporal's president Yang Shengjie grew from the size of a finger to about a hand. "Yesterday Once More" by The Carpenters began to play: "When I was young, I listen..."

The six or seven other people in the mag-lift looked at him oddly. Li hastily closed the box, whispering, "Sorry."

Exiting the elevator, he nodded politely at the endless

stream of his co-workers' faces. He passed through the crowded open-plan office, then the miniscule private offices of the middle managers. He stopped in front of his own office; the pupil-scanner quickly verified him as the occupant of the forty-square-meter space behind the door.

Li Huan walked into his office, and the door silently returned to its original position, merging into the wall. The gray room suddenly oozed with light: The ceiling turned bright blue within the time of a breath; the optical projector beamed white clouds upon it, which gathered and scattered, like swirling milk. The floor turned into a verdant patch of grass, the individual blades swaying gently wherever a foot was set, extending all the way to the walls. Those were now distant forests as far as the eye could reach.

Li sat in front of his desk, and started to inspect the box Little Xing had given him. "Yesterday Once More" began to play again, and the hand-sized President Yang seemed to be saying something, but Li wasn't paying attention—it couldn't be more than "thanks for all you've done for Fuxing Temporal," "the ages of Fuxing will commemorate your contributions," "no matter what kind of future you are in, you'll always be an important part of the Fuxing family," and other such pleasantries.

Instead, Li was absently gazing on the ball-cactus in a little pot on his desk. It was the only greenery in the room that was real, a gift brought by a German friend from his home country. Looking at it, Li couldn't help but start reflecting on his twenty-nine years of service at Fuxing Temporal.

He'd joined when he was thirty-three, and had progressed step by step, from a cramped workstation in the outer room to his own office. He had become one of the leading consultants in the temporal industry because of his day-in, day-out hard work. He was sixty-two this year; and aside from two round-trip vacations to the moon about twenty total days, he'd never been in cryostasis.

In this day and age, that kind of life was rare.

Ding-dong. The retro sound of the doorbell pulled Li's thoughts back to reality. As he stood up, the door that only opened for those with appointments parted automatically. Outside stood a woman, full of beauty and grace, except for her wan face and dark circles around her eyes.

Li greeted her: "Miss Su, please have a seat. I've waited a long time to meet you."

1.2

By 11 a.m., the Glittering Age lottery had been going on for three hours. The draw was done by computer and took place in groups, with five winners from each. These lucky few needed to pay a commitment fee and complete their pre-registration within twenty minutes. If they couldn't pay, or didn't have all the necessary information to fill the forms within the allotted time, the entrants forfeited their chance, and the next round would begin. Right now, the left half of the giant screen displayed five names from the ninth group, each name with a serial number from 41 to 45. None of them had dropped out yet.

As the emcee had previously explained, the fourth round of selections for the Glittering Age had temporal emigration terms of fifteen, twenty, twenty-five, thirty and sixty years. Each term had twenty spots. The right half of the screen showed the number of remaining spots for temporal emigrants in each category.

Oliver was tapping his fingers on his desk, drumming lightly with both hands. Roland looked at his friend, seeing the corners of his mouth moving, as if he was muttering something. He couldn't help but smile when he heard what Oliver was chanting.

"Deng Xiaoyong, Deng Xiaoyong, Deng Xiaoyong, Deng Xiaoyong..."

Deng Xiaoyong was Oliver's legal name. He and Roland both worked at a large multinational corporation, where English was the language of internal communication, and employees had to adopt English names. Oliver and Roland, who were also personal friends, had gotten into the habit outside of work.

"Oliver," Roland smiled. "You trying to use psychic powers to influence the draw?"

"It's almost the last round for the morning," Oliver retorted. "It's psychic powers or nothing."

"Aren't there still fifty places left in the afternoon draw?"

"There are fifty places total for the afternoon," said Oliver, as he pointed toward the main screen, "but only four left in the thirty-year category."

Roland studied the screen. Of the forty people who had been selected, sixteen had already taken the thirty-year option. Eleven had chosen twenty-five, five had chosen twenty, and seven had chosen fifteen; only one person had gone with the sixty-year option.

"It makes complete sense that thirty years would be the most popular option," Roland remarked.

"Yeah. The air will be better, the ecosystem will be more balanced, cities will have upgraded. All these things are long-term processes; I can't see them being accomplished any quicker than that. I mean, how cool is this? Go to sleep, skip the revolution, and wake up to a perfect new world."

Roland smiled and gave no reply. It was a matter of course that Oliver had faith in the future. Roland had no desire to argue with him, so instead took the conversation in a different direction. "Wasn't your pop pushing for the sixty-year option? How'd you talk him round?"

"The generation before us crossed the millennium, so they're really into the idea of crossing centuries. My mom and pop are always saying, with zv cryostasis technology maturing, they want to cross centuries one more time. I spent months dissecting the situation from every angle, and we had a couple of big fights." Oliver sighed, and continued. "In the end they gave in; maybe they think the changes after six decades will be too great. The future in thirty years will still have many traces of an age they are familiar with. After sixty years, that's not such a sure thing. If you migrate too far, no matter how good that place is, you'll never feel like it belongs to you, or that you belong to it."

"No matter how far a distance you go," Roland argued, "you can always find a road home. If you travel sixty years forward, though, you'll never be able to come back." So what's the fundamental difference, he wondered to himself, between thirty and sixty years?

"Actually, going forward ten years could be really good, too. After you wake up, some things will have advanced, and if you're satisfied, you can stay there, like a vacation. If you're not satisfied, you can freeze yourself for another eight, ten years. It's just too expensive to emigrate in short intervals. Some of us don't have the economic means for so much hassle," Oliver was sighing.

"If you're talking about truly settling down, then the twenty-five and thirty-year terms have the best cost-performance ratio. Speaking of which, was thirty years your idea or your girlfriend's?" asked Roland.

"It was mine; Jiajia still hasn't agreed to emigrate to the future."

"Shit, and you still came to the drawing?" Roland reflected that he himself didn't have the gall for this "do first, ask forgiveness later" approach. "You're so sure that after you set it up, you'll be able to convince her to emigrate to the future? And she'll be fine with you choosing thirty years?"

"There's so much great stuff in the future. Who wouldn't want to go, given the chance?" Oliver pouted. "I figure she's just afraid of the concept of being frozen for a few decades. Just like when airplanes first came out—a bunch of people were too afraid to fly, but later on they discovered it was quite safe, and people got over scaring themselves."

Just as he finished speaking, Oliver stood up, and threw his hands in the air, his face registering triumph and disbelief, like a goalie who'd just nailed a last-minute save.

Roland looked up at the stage. The screen read: "46 – Deng Xiaoyong."

3.2

Su Bu took a seat in front of Li Huan's desk, and brushed her hair off her face. She saw Li was looking at her. That wasn't at all strange; she was a very attractive woman, and her appearance always drew stares, like ants to honey. What was strange was that, when Li looked at her, his eyes were simply seeing, not feasting on her. Su cleared her throat with purpose; whether thirty years back or thirty years in the future, no pretty woman wants an old man lustily gazing upon her. But what she disliked even more was an old man looking at her with eyes completely devoid of desire.

Li blushed as he smiled. "Miss Su, I loved watching your films when I was younger. I'm an old man, but when I see you looking the exact same as you did on the screen, I can't help but feel like all these years I lived actually haven't passed me by. It must seem funny to you."

"I'm honored by your kindness."

After these brief pleasantries, Li turned to the actual topic at hand. "My team has already completed the analysis report. We hope it will provide you with solid information to consult when making your decision about emigrating further." A projection panel popped out of Li's desk. Li extended his hand and made a few swipes in front of the projection, and the virtual forests on the wall facing Su turned into a report full of graphics and text. Li tapped a few more times on the projection panel, and graphics flowed around the screen to form a new report in front of his client.

"Thank you," Su took control of the report display and browsed its contents quickly. As she looked it over, Li commented concisely on the content displayed at each stage. "Over the course of the decade, the aftershocks of the temporal bubble and financial crisis will gradually fade. The global economy will recover. Today, we can objectively state that the benefits of the development of temporal technology outweigh the costs to humanity. Rather than us acclimatizing to the future, it has allowed us to choose our futures...

"According to the assessments made by our company's external experts in regard to extraterrestrial exploration, finding clean energy solutions using new extraterrestrial energy sources within the next fifty years is impracticable, based upon the high cost and difficulty of survey and transport...

"Assuming the major world economies' continued compliance with the Treaty, in another hundred years, the Earth's ecological equilibrium index can be restored to the value it had at the start of this century...

"In 2048, researchers at the University of Edinburgh discovered that the main cryostasis technology used by the global temporal industry could only maintain zero vital-sign stasis for about forty-two years. After forty-two years, depending on the individual's metabolism, subjects age between 1.7 and 2.3 years for each decade passed in stasis. In 2049, China passed the Temporal Emigration Act, Article 11, Paragraph 3 of which stipulates that planning documents for long-term cryostasis for a period of longer than forty years are not permitted to use 'zero-vital sign stasis' or related terms. Paragraph 4 states that for a cryostasis period of forty or more years, planning documents must use 'low volatile sign cryostasis' in their descriptions, and clearly state that those in cryostasis will experience some natural aging."

By the time he finished explaining, Su had swiped through the whole report. Then Li Huan asked the question: "With our current level of technology, under the conditions of LVS cryostasis, if you went under for a century, taking metabolic differences into account, you would age between eight and eleven years. Considering this, do you still want to emigrate one hundred years into the future?"

3.3

Su Bu pursed her lips tightly, but when she spoke, she didn't answer Li Huan's question. "I heard that in 2049, the government required tempo firms to wake up all clients who had signed up to do cryo for longer than four decades."

"That is correct. Due to the huge amounts of compensation offered and the crisis of confidence, we had a market panic, which led to the collapse of the temporal bubble, as well as an economic crisis. That was the darkest page in the history of the temporal industry."

"What I want to say is, those who got woken up were lucky." Su spoke quietly. "They had time to adjust to the world falling apart. They didn't have to wake up full of hope and extravagant wishes, only to discover that reality was a nightmare."

Li didn't know what to say.

Su continued: "Mr. Li, can you tell me something? You

worked in the temporal industry all these years—how could you remain calm? How did you resist the temptation to emigrate?"

This question was unexpected; Li shook his head awkwardly. "Actually, although I never personally agreed with skipping so much time into the future, when the emigration craze first started, I was no match for my wife's enthusiasm, and went with a friend to a bunch of lotteries."

"And then?"

"In the end, my friend finally got his wish, and won a spot in the thirty-year scheme. I wasn't so lucky. However, through attending those VIP events, I discovered a promising industry, so I quit my old job and signed up to join the temporal guys. After that, I had my second, then third child. I was busy with work; I didn't have time for temporal emigration. So, just like people of the previous generations, I let my life go on in step with the passage of time. Before I knew it, my kids were grown, and I was old."

Li laughed at himself, and at that moment glanced at the picture on his desk of him with his wife and children. His smile became peaceful and content. "Speaking of that friend, he should be revived from cryostasis this year. I'm old enough to be his father now."

Su laughed along, but when her smile faded, the exhaustion and worry were hard to conceal. "I've thought it over, and eight years is fine, or ten, whatever. As long as I can leave this era, I'm willing to do what it takes."

Li sighed, and gave Su the pre-filled contract. He hesitated for a second, and then spoke: "Speaking not as a temporal emigration consultant, but a person with life experiences...I don't actually recommend buying such a temporal emigration plan. If you think about it rationally, you might find that this age isn't as bad as you think. It's not worth paying ten years of your life to escape."

Su looked around at the verdant landscape projected in Li's office, and thought about the all-encompassing sandstorm outside. She thought she'd had enough of a world of the virtual and the desolate.

She shook her head: "With all due respect, you have no idea what a letdown this is for someone who was in cryostasis for three decades."

"Yes, but who can say that the world a century later will live up to expectations?"

"But if I do nothing, then nothing will change." Su no longer looked at Li, but lowered her head to sign the contract: "Su Bu, May 20, 2068."

2.0

Li Huan sat in the corner of a café next to a window. He selected a latte and a half-portion of onion rings on a tablet, and swiped over to the payment step. He took off his glasses and covered his right eye with his hand, gazing into the device's camera with his left. It quickly read his pupil. "Payment complete," read the message on the screen.

As Li waited for his coffee and onion rings, he looked absentmindedly out the window. He didn't notice when the waiter brought him his food and drink. Beijing in April was warm and pleasant, all billowing clouds and blue skies, and catkins floating in the air. The window reflected a young man who was playing the piano in the café; as his fingers floated across the keyboard and built up the chords, the image blurred before Li's eyes, as if it were a trick of the light.

The pianist was playing something classical; Li couldn't tell if it was Mozart or Schubert. His wife once summed up his relationship with classical music in a few words: listens a lot, understands nothing. Li had come to like classical more and more in recent years. Ever since the turn of the millennium, the unstoppable tide of digitization seemed to have replaced printed photos and books with touchscreens overnight. Yet the black and white keys of the piano were an exceptional pairing; their clear sounds seemed to stand guard over the lengthening shadows of an earlier age.

Lost in thought, Li was jolted by a discordant note, like someone speaking within the music, calling a name over and over. It sounded like "Roland."

"Roland!"

The new arrival patted Li on his shoulder. Li snapped back to reality, and raising his gaze, he saw Oliver sitting down at the table across from him.

"What's up with you? I called your name over and over, and you didn't respond." Oliver placed a mug on the table, grinning.

"My new workplace didn't buy into the English name thing," Li smiled back. "Nobody's called me that for years. It's a been a few years, bro, huh?"

"Three years. After you quit, man, and got into the tempo game, we haven't gone drinking once. Just that half a game of badminton one time." Oliver's voice held a little reproach. "If I wasn't going in the freezer the day after tomorrow, I probably couldn't have gotten an appointment with you, busy man."

Li, embarrassed, scratched his head. "Work's been really busy."

"Speaking of work, I really don't get you, man. You jump ship to do tempo, yet you don't want to emigrate yourself. It's 2042, man! It's like doing finance and not buying stocks...or doing film and not boning the actresses."

"Hey, now! Actually, I've always thought things are quite good as they are; who knows what the future will be like? Sometimes, when I'm advising clients, in my heart I feel like telling them not to do it." As he spoke, he noticed Oliver's wedding ring: "So she's willing to go after all?"

Oliver didn't understand the question at first, until he saw Li gazing on his left hand with raised eyebrows. He absently rubbed the ring with his left thumb, and answered awkwardly: "Uh, yeah, it's all good. But it's not Jiajia."

Li was a bit confused. Oliver had gotten married, so how could his bride not be Jiajia?

But then—hadn't Oliver said that Jiajia was unwilling to go into cryostasis? Or maybe, what made her reluctant wasn't just the cryostasis, but also the prospect of skipping twenty-six years into an unknown future?

3.4

Li Huan had seen Su Bu out, and was packing his personal belongings in the office. As he put each item in the cardboard box, he felt like he was organizing a stack of old yellowed photographs—snapshots of constant departures and arrivals over half a lifetime.

Whether it was at the end of the thirties or the start of the forties, when the global temporal emigration craze was at its height—or the present day, when hordes of people were rushing to beat a mad path to an even more distant future—Li still felt he wanted to live his life in the normal time plane. This belief for life is what had doomed him to never be able to love his job as a temporal consultant. That said, he didn't dislike his job.

In his twenty-nine years with Fuxing Temporal, he'd seen the collapse of the bubble, the climate crises, and countless clients' hopes and optimism turn to disappointment and fright. In these dysphoric times, the job of temporal consultant had given Li peace and serenity. He never sold his clients the idea of a perfect future. It might have been for this very reason that he had become one of the most respected and trusted consultants in the industry.

Finally, his possessions were in the box. Li smoothed back his white hair, and said to himself, "Now, you're really retiring."

It occurred to him that it was progress and transformation which pushed forth the wheels of history, but what made a person smile in the recollection of their life was love and quietude.

Li thought again of Su Bu, who had just left, and how, when she'd asked her question, he'd talked about that friend of his. He remembered when he'd said goodbye to that friend in the café, twenty-six years prior.

The two of them had sipped their coffees silently, until Oliver asked: "Some time ago, I read a book by Thomas Mann. The guy wrote, 'We now know that belief in the future as a 'better world' is a fallacy created by the scholars of progress.' You and Jiajia, who aren't willing to emigrate to the future—is that what you also believe?"

"Hm? Fallacies by scholars of progress? I hadn't thought about it that deeply."

Now, Li Huan wanted to tell Oliver, "I'm not willing to

emigrate to the future, simply because I've already found love and quietude in the present."

That time, Li Huan and Oliver had talked of many things, long into the night. When parting, Oliver had gripped Li's shoulder, his voice regretful as he said, "We're brothers who've gone drinking together, played badminton together, pulled all-nighters together. Take care. If you change your contact info, remember to send me an email; let's get together again in twenty-six years!"

"Today, you call me 'brother,'" Li rejoined, smiling. "Next time we meet, I'll be twenty-six years older than you—you'll be calling me 'uncle.'"

His goodbyes said, Li Huan ambled alone through the empty streets, as the frosty moonlight spilled over the willow branches. The sound of the piano from the distant café was ceaseless, like the passage of time. ▪

AUTHOR'S NOTE

In writing this story, I intended not to explicate the cutting-edge technological developments mentioned in the text, but rather, to shed light on how the ongoing process of modernization will influence humanity. As you might have realized, the story was inspired by the current situation of urban China's real-estate markets.

MA ER 马耳

Ma Er lives in Guiling, Guangxi Zhuang Autonomous Region, and is the founder and editor of online literary magazine Shikongliu (《时空流》, Streams of Time and Space). Ma mixes ancient myth with modern imagery and writes with clarity and sophistication. His simple but exacting use of words constructs a world of fable, fantasy, and reality. "Streams of time and Space" is also a literary theory proposed originally by Ma that by studying the past, projecting the future, and ultimately focusing on the present, a writer breaks the rigid boundaries of time and space to achieve a more fluid understanding of the unique characteristics of the era.

CRANE

鶴

He let his head hang. That way, he could better think about certain things. He could see the skin below his chest and a large section of shining white floor. The brightness did all it could not to draw any attention, but it still stirred an anxiety within him. He noticed his skin had formed excessive slack, as if in that instant he had aged ten years—a direct reaction to the bright rays.

He entered the inner room, abandoning the brightness behind him. He knew that, with each step he took, the glow would fade by a degree, until all that remained was darkness. Far in the interior of the room, heavy flannel curtains blocked out all the rays. Clouds of dust floated down and gathered in the corners. This further obstructed the refraction of rays, which would find themselves immobilized, as if bound with rope.

Naturally, the darkest place was inaccessible. The crane standing in the corner of the room held its head high. Its black eyes were profound and serene and following them deeper led to the darkness's last dwelling. For the moment, he could only stand at the exterior of that lodging, peering inside with curiosity and a little greed.

The crane flapped its wings. Why it did so was not apparent, but it looked irritated. It had stood there a long time and usually had the patience to adjust to his presence. But, slowly, it flapped its wings and began to fly around the room. He stood below, somewhat terrified. The crane expanded. It grew so large that the room could no longer tolerate it. The crane's two wings and head extended out of the walls so that now it was transporting the room on its body as it flew.

He recalled that fantastic event, and thought that perhaps what was happening was that event. In truth, he could not see what was happening outside. The crane's body barricaded the view. He could only imagine the crane carrying the room on its body as it flew. The crane now engulfed the room. He was buried in dense feathers. Its hot flesh was right above his head. It was, admittedly, an unbearable taste and feeling. He only hoped the crane would land quickly or would swell until the room burst. That way he could fall to the ground amidst a dazzling new field of view.

Thinking of his room, he was reluctant to let it go. It was a pretty room. Its appeal was not only the beauty of its decor and design, but the outdoors, a splendid piece of scenery. Nowadays, there were few of these stand-alone houses with beautiful views available. In truth, he could not even remember where else he had seen a house exactly like this one: a stand-alone structure facing an open plain with a cluster of mountains in the distance. He could also not remember how he had acquired it—had he bought it? Had he rented it? No recollection surfaced from the ocean of his thoughts. He just knew that every day, from daybreak to nightfall, he had leaned out of that window to gaze at the scenery with nobody coming to bother him. It was as if the surrounding population didn't exist. He had also never experienced such anxiety—to him, as long as the house and the scenery remained, all would be fine. People were not important.

Now he fretted about where the crane would fly. He knew it had to land someplace. He didn't know where it would land, or how long it would stay there. He also didn't know if it would bring the house along when it left again. He concluded his anxiety stemmed from the fear of a new place. He didn't know what kind of place it would take him to. If he didn't like the place then it was probable his whole life was lost.

The crane finally let some space into the room. He could put his head out the window to look around. Most of the time he only saw white clouds whooshing by. Sometimes he saw a bird or two brushing past his window. The crane appeared to have a disdainful disregard for these birds, whose frames and appearance were awkward by comparison. In any case, he didn't see any signs of agitation. The crane just flapped its wings, silently casting its shadow over the other birds. In an instant, it had flown past them and was rushing into the next layer of clouds.

The crane's flight patterns were as follows: In the morning and evening it would fly low, as though it was tired or testing the limits of its laziness. Only at noon, when the weather was at its clearest, would it fly to the maximum altitudes. Up high, temperatures were frigid and the air was restless. He mostly huddled up in a corner of the room and shuddered as he looked out the window at the clouds sweeping past. But up high, clouds were actually rather scarce. He mostly had to rely on his instincts to guess what was happening outside—there was an oil lamp on the table, and even though it was securely mounted, the flickering of the flame explained to him the crane's turbulent path. He mostly watched the prancing flame and imagined the flying crane, its body sloping upward as it climbed and its wings not beating as it glided on a rising current. It only needed to follow the ascending flow; that was all. But still, its body couldn't avoid making violent tremors and so the wings were required to act as a stabilizing mechanism. They looked like two kites doing their best to maintain relative stability as the crane rocked to the left and to the right, allowing it to sail, ever soaring through the air. This beautiful flight looked just like a dance, but one that involved tremendous risk.

He understood that flying at this height was necessary—
the crane was approaching a blockade constructed of many
mountains. Only by catching the rising air currents could
it make it over the rows of summits. But by instinct he preferred flying at low altitudes. That was when he could free
himself from the fetters of angst and lean out of the window
into the screaming winds to scan the distance. He could see
plains, rivers, ponds, and low hills, and never grew tired of
looking at these things.

Once in a while there were people on the hills, standing
there like statues—always a lone figure. That moved him
and reminded him of himself. So he stretched out of the
window as far as he could to get a closer look, but he never
saw more than a fuzzy silhouette. He couldn't tell if that
person could see him—this spectacle of a huge bird carrying a house. It was likely that nobody could miss it.

But that was not certain. Even as the crane flew lower it
was still far from the ground and the people on the hills
still only looked like little black and white spots. They
would not be able to tell what kind of bird this was, much
less perceive the house it carried. There were moments
when he felt strange. He could not understand what he had
become—a cartoon character, or some pitiful creature living in a dream within reality. He might not be any better
than parasitic lice lodged in bird feathers; even though his
senses were cognizant of far more than those of a louse.

The crane's occasional landings were uneventful. Most of the time it landed in barren swamplands. Sometimes he didn't even dare leave the house. He was afraid that the ants crawling out of the swamps would bite him to death. Some of the better landings, on waterfronts, were nonetheless lifeless scenes. The shores and water were strewn with the white bones of animal carcasses. The landing he remembered best was on the edge of a clear stream. He caught a shiny, silver fish in his hands and played with it. The crane walked over, stretched out its neck and pecked the fish out of his palms. It put the fish on the ground and pecked it a few more times. It kept pecking it until it was bloody and raw, but didn't even eat it.

When they took flight, he stayed in the window to watch the fish. It had long died, but it appeared to him to have transformed into another kind of animal—a kind of nameless, immortal life form. What he saw transpire was evidence of this: When the crane had just taken off, he saw it was a bloody fish with its tangled entrails showing. As the crane climbed, the scene gradually changed. A new form emerged from within the dead fish. It was no longer a repulsive red and black carcass. It appeared as an abstract black and red shape. The crane created a new kind of life. His anger toward the bird quickly dissipated.

At night, in the dark, he would often wonder: had he become the crane's prisoner? The slave image lingered in his thoughts, causing his sleep to become restless. The crane never opened its mouth or said a word, but from its black, opaque eyes he could discern that it was thinking. What it thought—he couldn't know.

One evening, they landed in a patch of weeds. Deep in the night, he heard the crane crying in pain. He woke to it rocking violently and in the confusion he leapt out of the window.

Just then, the commotion stopped. He saw the crane trembling and slanted to the ground with a mangled lump of bloody flesh at its rear end.

At daybreak, he saw that it was a bird with a build similar to that of the crane. But its body was much smaller and it did not appear to be the product of birth, as it did not have the form of a newly hatched chick, even though there was blood spattered all over the crane's backside.

This time they rested for a few days. The crane needed time to regain its strength. It was the longest he had spent on land since they had first taken flight, and he was thrilled. He scoured a nearby piece of land and climbed every hill he could reach. He discovered a maze of narrow trails that crisscrossed through the hills and wilderness but never found out where they led. Every time he followed a trail for a certain distance, a powerful force would grip him and urge him to go back to where he came from. Perhaps he was afraid to leave any signs of the crane too far behind.

When the crane finally took flight again, he noticed that

the small trails formed the huge image of a bird. They were actually one trail, with no beginning or end that meandered through the hills and wilderness, continually crossing and parting as if it were some kind of disorganized game.

So all that searching had been in vain. He had to be pleased that he hadn't explored the trails any further, even if he felt a faint regret. He wondered if perhaps things on the ground were different.

During this flight, the crane changed. It shrunk a little. This opened up even more room in his house and obviously that was a good thing, but he began to question it. Their journey continued, but now covered in a shadow of uncertainty. He needed to think hard about this.

He truly desired to know where the crane was flying to, but of the things he could learn, that was the least likely. Of all his options, the best choice was to lean out of the window and watch the crane for long periods of time. The crane rarely lowered its head to look at him and he did his best not to alarm it. But he would study its every movement with more care: every flap of its wings and the gentle turning of its long neck.

It was getting smaller and smaller now. After a month it was only two thirds of its previous size. That slowed its speed and tamed its movements. He sat in the room and could feel his chest swelling. It felt like there was something that was going to burst from inside him.

One day, as his chest ballooned, tremors shook the house. He ran to the window and looked outside anxiously. The room was approaching the ground. The crane was preparing to land. It was only noon. The crane had never landed at this time of day before.

Outside, uneven shadows swayed across his window. A few days earlier, he had experienced a vague premonition and covered his window with a piece of translucent bamboo paper in order to keep out any outside rays or scenery.

After another violent tremor, the house landed on the ground. The shadows outside grew more distinct. A few of them gathered on the glass, effusing a red-white hue. Familiar sounds and voices entered the room. Even if he had long forgotten them, the last thing he wanted to hear at that moment was those sounds and voices. Still, they crept in through every crack in the house. He could almost see their faces: small, tapered faces with sparse white beards on the edges. When a wind blew they floated around his room, floating into every corner. He sulked in his room for the rest of the day. In the evening, the sounds and voices drifted away and everything fell silent.

He slowly opened the window and saw an avenue of cold light that was wide and as straight as a pen. It had a mirror-like surface made of glossy stone tiles that stretched into the distance. On either side there were countless low houses in a build similar to his. They all had their lights out, only allowing clean moon rays to sprinkle the edges of their roofs.

He jumped from the window as softly as he could and climbed up the crane's belly, slowly making his way onto its back. He then followed its curved neck all the way to its long, sharp beak.

The crane opened its eyes. From atop the beak, he looked into them and saw a plain stretching infinitely. The crane stood up. Towering above the road and houses, it began to gently beat its wings. He saw two dried leaves starting to whirl around its body. They were huge, solid, and looked as though if they were to strike him it would be fatal. He gripped the crane's beak firmly.

The crane slowly rose. A whirlwind pounded against him and shattered the two dry leaves. He could see the shinning road start to narrow. The outlines of a city appeared underneath him, and then gradually dissolved from his sight.

On this flight, he was deathly cold and saw high mountains up close for the first time. As they passed over them, the crane tilted its wings and looked like an arrow flying at an upward angle shooting past the jagged peaks. Terrified and thrilled he crawled onto the crane's back and lowered himself into its feathers for warmth. He heard loud blasts ringing around his ears, as if there was a giant foot kicking him over and over. Eventually he slid down the crane's feathers like a drop of water and returned into the house.

After that, the crane continued shrinking. Its flying became increasingly unsteady. Every so often it would drop vertically from the air and land in a bustling neighborhood or at the mouth of a tall chimney. He also endured the shadows endlessly returning to sway on his window, the blaring city sounds and frightening gloom. The farther ahead they flew, the denser the city became. It was also getting larger.

He felt as though he had reached the end of a road. The boundary was the closed window that would either open to a straight passageway or a deep chasm. Actually, the passage and the chasm were the same. The passage was a level trap, the chasm a vertical road.

There was a problem. He couldn't open the window. As long as the shadows remained, he was like a mouse backed into the corner of the room who could only slip out late in the night. The city blocks they landed in were always filled with a maze of roads running in all directions and chasms surrounded the chimney mouths. The strange thing was that no matter where they were, daytime was constantly filled with shadows. It was as though they existed in every corner the sunlight reached. It was only by flying into the sky that their presence could be escaped.

The torment lingered, and the crane continued shrinking. Eventually, one day he discovered it had returned to its original size. It could only fly around in the room. Having lost the crane's support, the house dropped and shaved the dense crowns of a few trees before it made a smooth landing.

At first, everything was a quiet and that brought him some relief. But soon he started to see the many long and short shadows on his window. Their familiar sounds and voices seeped into the room, attacking him from all directions.

Feeling wretched, he was determined not to leave the room. Even at nightfall he wouldn't open the window. He imagined it would be a grisly, hellish world. All he hoped was for the crane to return to its giant form and rise off with the room once more. But the crane had resumed its old habits. It fluttered around the room, showing no trace of its transformation.

So, they were each other's prisoner. The crane could not take him flying and he could not let it fly away. He sat dumbstruck on his bed, gaping at the wall, when the crane leapt up beside him. Now it was the crane that made the effort to observe him. It tilted its head, locking one glossy black eye with his. It suffused a small cold light that filled his field of vision and then transformed into a glittering gem. He could now only see the layer of gleam on the eye's surface and was no longer able to look into it. The two were left to face one another in silence. He closed his eyes and everything went black. He opened them and his big eyes met with its little eye. Occasionally, the crane would take off mischievously, causing the house to jump off the ground and send him a jolt of surprise. Once the excitement passed, the days felt longer and even more miserable.

Seeing the crane standing at the head of his bed entranced in stillness, he was able to relax and return to his own thoughts. He watched the shadows outside his window slanting and getting longer by the day. He knew that some unavoidable changes had taken place. The shifting outside and stagnation inside piled together, deepening his anxiety. He worried that in the days ahead that critical point would be reached and he would be forced to open the window.

He sat in distress, with much time passing until his thoughts had hardened. He noticed a long, hard beak sticking out beneath his eyes. He barely sensed it. The change felt natural. It was not until his neck and body had grown thick plumage that he was startled. But by then the process was irreversible. He stood in front of the dressing mirror day after day, watching the transformation in hysteria, stretching his unfledged wings into the room and flapping them. At the other end, the crane stood at the head of the bed watching him with its glossy black eyes. It had a pure yet arrogant air as it observed this person who resembled it more by the day.

In the end, he transformed into a crane. And one day he used his inflated body to take the house flying. The first time he went up he had climbed high, for he rushed to pass every cloud he saw. Some time later, he was picked up by a rising air current and soared even higher. He saw a mountain towering before him.

The current rushed him along. High ground flew towards him. Only now did he perceive the danger. But it was too late. The current thrust him at the wall of the mountain. The house shattered. He saw a swarm of debris and furniture plunging to the ground behind him. Within the mass he saw the large dressing mirror and his reflection diving to the ground behind him. Inside the reflection he saw the large dressing mirror and his reflection inside it—one distraught, tumbling man.

As he fell, he was thinking:

What happened to that crane? ▪

AUTHOR'S NOTE

I loved flying as a kid and have read many stories about it. The Greek myth of Icarus flying through the sky on the wax wings of Daedalus was the one that impressed me the most, which is probably the inspiration for this story. The crane is also my favorite bird, an ethereal creature—apathetic and mysterious. The man in the story is a modern figure trying to hold on to an ancient myth. He is hesitant and weak but never loses hope completely; instead, he continues to try new possibilities. In the end, the house is broken and the man falls to ground, rendering him a modern man again—a pitiful but inevitable end.

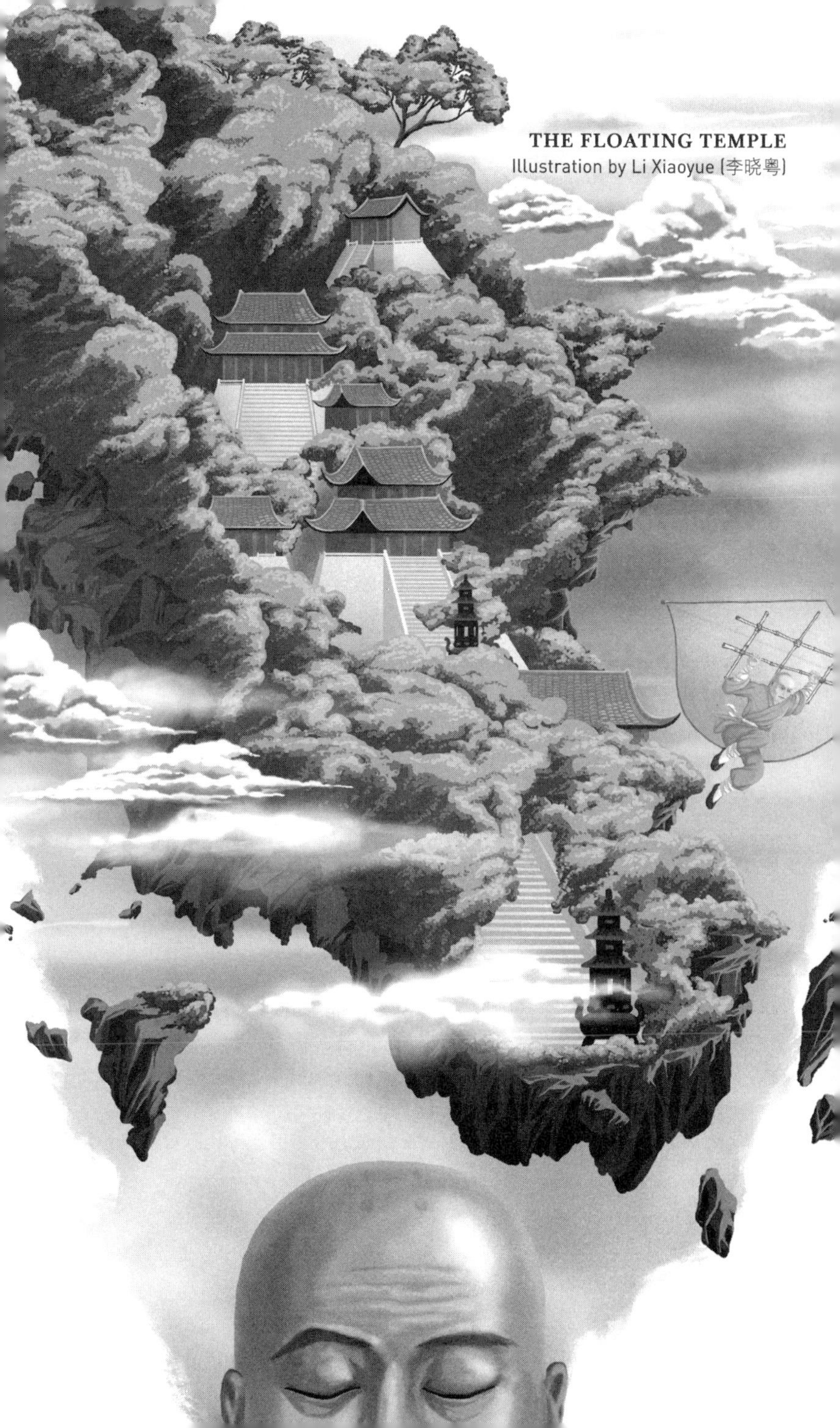

THE FLOATING TEMPLE
Illustration by Li Xiaoyue (李晓粤)

QITONGREN 骑桶人

While some Chinese fantasy writers are criticized for imitating their supposedly more mature Western counterparts, the Bucket Rider (Qitongren) or Li Qiqing (李启庆) turned to ancient myths, legends, and traditional images for inspiration. Founder of online fantasy magazine Jiuge (《九歌》), Li has published a short story collection, a full-length novel, a historical account of ancient Chinese fantasy literature, and a biography of the famous Chinese Buddhist monk, Master Hong Yi. His fantasy writings are said to have inherited the spirit of fantasy literature from the Tang (618-907) and Song (960-1279) dynasties.

SPRING AT DONGKE TEMPLE

东柯僧院的春天

Forty kilometers away from Qingcheng County stands the Dongke Mountain. With its high altitude and thick forest cover, the mountain is virtually trackless. Legend has it that the Dongke Temple is somewhere on the mountain. The monks, however, have all become *anāgāmin* ("non-returner," practitioners who have reached the penultimate stage to becoming Arhats), and therefore extinguished all earthly desires. A few decades ago, a woodsman accidentally found the temple and dwelled there for several days. He returned, yet remained tight-lipped about the experience. Finally, on his deathbed, the woodsman vaguely mentioned the "many swallows in the temple." He went on to say that despite his pleasant stay, it would be better for his family to "never seek the temple again."

On a spring day in the year 808, scholar Liu Xichu took a boat with seven or eight of his comrades up the stream to Dongke Mountain in search of the legendary temple. They found the source of the stream, only to discover untrodden woods and dark ravines. Soon, the sun began to set, alarming the scholars who urged the boatman to go back. The boatman, however, was not used to navigating the mountain stream and steered the boat into a rock, where it foundered. The current, though not deep, was swift, and Liu had to grasp the branch of an old tree. When he finally managed to lift his head above the water to search for his companions, they were long gone—their faint cries for help gradually fading away. In the end, only the chirps of the birds and roar of the apes echoing in the woods remained, a heart-wrenching and miserable sound at the time.

Liu breathed deeply and took a brief moment to collect himself. He crawled onto the bank along the branch. Walking around, he found an old tree to climb up and rest. Thankfully, a piece of *nang* bread was still safely tucked in his robe. Though it was soaking wet and had become soft, he tore off a piece and swallowed it. By this time it was dark and the moon had begun rising against the mountain. Liu, thinking of his family, couldn't help shedding a few tears.

The next morning, Liu climbed down the tree and tried to find his way back, gradually losing all sense of time and direction. Every piece of mountain rock and every branch of every tree looked exactly the same. He lived on wild fruits when he finished the *nang* bread. His wanderings became slow and tired, until finally, he fell down at the foot of an old tree, exhausted, not able even to stir a limb.

"I can't believe I'm going to die here!" he said to himself.

On seeing a few mountain flowers dancing in the wind not far away, he began sobbing wildly. By dusk, he ceased crying and felt much better; his strength seemed to have returned. Standing up and looking around, he began collecting fruit for dinner. Suddenly, he noticed a faint scent of flowers in the wind.

He was carried away by the scent and carefully followed it. The moon was bright and the wind refreshing. Liu Xichu kept walking till midnight, using reserves of strength he didn't know he had. The fragrance became rich and pure, sometimes sweet and intoxicating like good wine, sometimes sharp and piercing like a blade. Enchanted, Liu kept advancing unconsciously into a valley. In the moonlight, he entered an ancient forest with giant trees several arm-lengths wide. No wild grass was found on the ground, just a layer of gray. The fragrance was beyond a mere scent now, but became like a flowing spring.

Liu stumbled forward, suddenly noticing a shabby temple. The front gate collapsed a long time ago. There was an azalea tree, three meters tall, in front of the ruined gate. Despite the dim light, he could still see the vivid colors of its branches.

Liu entered the temple shouting: "Is anyone here? Anyone?" Only a faint humming came as reply. Though he walked the whole night, only at this very moment did he notice his feet aching to the bone. He dropped to the ground, at first sitting, then later sliding down and falling into a deep sleep.

He awoke the next morning to a courtyard full of wild grass. Inside the main hall, spiderwebs were draped everywhere. On the beams and pillars were stacks of swallow nests. A few Buddha statues were barely upright with broken arms or missing eyes, their heads covered with gray bird droppings.

Liu Xichu was so starved, he was light-headed. After searching inside and outside the temple, he found a few berries that were sour and sharp, which he gulped down nevertheless. Only when he felt better did he notice that there seemed to be many birds flying above the forest—their wings rustling together. He left the temple and labored to the top of the mountain. Endless bird droppings covered the ground. He managed to collect some forest fruit and saw a wild beehive. He started a fire to smoke-out the bees, and fed himself a hearty meal of honey, before continuing to march upwards. Fortunately, the mountain top was not so far. He moved upward, step by step. A swallow would sweep by from time to time and then lightly fly through the leaves, up into the sky.

It was still morning when he left the temple, but by the time he reached the top it was sunset. The sun shone through the mountain peak on the opposite side and tinged half the valley in deep red, leaving the other half dark green. Countless swallows swarmed back and forth above the woods. When they flew into the sunshine, they became like the flaming birds of Zhu Rong—the fire god—a blaze of red all through. But once they were in the dark half, they turned into green fish, as if swiftly swimming underwater.

The moon was bright and stars scarce when Liu arrived back at the temple. He made do by dozing off and eating some of the honey acquired the day before. He brightened up again, carefully examining the temple inside and out. Though in ruins, much of the temple's richly ornamented columns, beams, green rafters, and red tiles remained. Judging by its scale, the temple could have housed more than a hundred monks; the state of its decay was curious.

There were swallow nests everywhere, from the main hall right through to the dining room; the abbot's chamber, and even the toilet, were occupied by birds. The floor, covered by their droppings over the years, seemed soft when Liu first set upon them, but were solid as stone at their core.

Swallows flew into the temple from time to time to feed their young, not in the least affected by Liu's presence. Maybe they were accustomed to the monks here before; the sudden appearance of a human didn't seem to alarm them.

Liu lived on honey for several days in the temple—becoming, surprisingly, too happy to think of home. In the swallow nests lay many eggs, but Liu was not willing to eat them. When the honey was finished, he went into the woods to pick wild fruit. Though they were only half-ripe, Liu didn't mind their bitter taste.

Just like that, over ten days passed until one day at noon, Liu heard a vague rustle behind one of the Buddha figures. Turning to check, he found a deep pit in the ground. It was too dark inside to see anything. On the nearby wall there was also a large hole from where the rustling noise seemed to be originating. Liu bent down to examine the hole close-ly and got a feeling that some kind of monster must be hiding there. He grabbed a stick and poked inside. Suddenly, a bat soared and crashed into his face, leaving him confused and somewhat disturbed. Another bat was barely out of the hole when Liu hastily jumped aside. More dark brown bats flipped their webbed wings, scrambling to make out the opening. In a blink of an eye, these bats clouded the main hall, rendering it in a dull darkness.

Only an hour later did all bats leave the hole, gliding out of the main hall to form a long line. Before Liu could recover from his shock, he heard breathing from the pit. Startled, Liu found a piece of brick and threw it into the pit from afar.

"Argh!" A scream came from the bottom, sounding like a person.

Liu then groped the edge, shouting back: "Are you a person or a ghost?" Some babbling rose from the pit. Liu listened for a while and guessed it must be a request: "Pull me up." As he extended a long stick down into the pit, someone grabbed it as he expected. With much effort, Liu pulled the person out of the pit. He was stunned when his eyes met the person.

He was unkempt, all skin and bones with the exception of a bulging belly. On seeing Liu, the man called out with great joy.

Liu collected wild fruits for the man, who lowered his head to smell them but refused to take any. Instead, the man grabbed a handful of dirt and offered it to Liu. Liu shook his head and went to the forest spring to get water for the man to clean himself. After washing, it seemed the man was very old, with long thick eyebrows and white hair. It was probably due to the sedentary, immobile life he had spent in the pit, but his feet were both shriveled. His skin was sickly pale due to sunlight deprivation; the many freckles on his body only served to add to the weirdness of the man's appearance.

But there's something even more unusual about the man: when he first climbed out of the pit, he was overjoyed; now, he suddenly seemed stiff, like he was indifferent to and unmoved by everything and everyone in the world. He had gone blind due to the long lasting darkness, but his hearing was acute. Liu discovered the only thing that interested the old man was the beating wings and singing of the swallows. Whenever a swallow flew inside, he would slowly turn his head to follow the slightest flapping sound, with a mysterious smile at the corner of his lips. Liu sat with him for an entire afternoon, surprisingly discovering that the old man seemed to be able to distinguish each and every swallow.

Every time one of them flew into the main hall, he would turn in the direction of its nest, listening to their twittering, as if he could understand them.

He also seemed to live off the dirt. The deep pit could very well have been the result of his own digging. Sometimes, he appeared to wake from a dream and regain a moment of consciousness. At those times, he would speak to Liu with eagerness. But Liu couldn't understand most of it, only vaguely learning that the old man was the abbot of the temple, with the Dharma name "Wushi." Still, Liu was patient. He went out everyday to look for wild fruit and sat down with Wushi to leisurely appreciate the sounds made by the swallows. Gradually, Liu became intoxicated as well: the ethereal swallows gliding across the hollow main hall, their wings flapping as if they were a refreshing spring born of mountain rock. They landed in their own nests, singing so softly and elegantly that Liu believed it more beautiful than even the finest music ever created by man.

Over time, he was able to follow Wushi, who was indeed the abbot of Dongke Temple. More than a decade ago, when the temple was undisturbed, all the monks kept their minds on Buddhist practice, hoping one day to become an Arhat or even reach Nirvana. One spring, many swallows arrived unexpectedly. They started to build nests and breed. The merciful Buddhists naturally let the birds be and never interfered. By autumn, all the swallows took off.

But the next spring brought even more of them. Ripples were set in the formerly peaceful hearts of the monks; some became addicted to the flapping of wings and the singing of the birds, believing them to be more immensely delightful than any Buddhist teachings.

By the third year, on a dewy morning, a monk transformed into a swallow and flew away. It was the year that the stray woodsman came to stay. Wushi asked for him to be sent back and instructed that nothing should ever come out of his mouth—he was afraid that people would flood into the temple on hearing of the strange event and disturb the monks' practice.

By spring of the fourth year, when the swallows returned once more, half the monks in the temple transformed into swallows and simply flew away. By the fifth year, all had become swallows except Wushi, who was left alone in the empty temple.

Despair prevailed in Wushi's mind. He no longer meditated or recited scripture, only idly sitting in the main hall, digging and eating dirt from the ground when he was hungry. Over a decade later, a deep pit had developed, and he was trapped inside. He couldn't get out even if he wanted to. Having sat in the dark for such a long time, his eyesight had completely gone, but his hearing improved more and more over time. He began to take an interest in the flapping and singing of the swallows. He too felt that they were far more enchanting than any Buddhist teaching, especially when the baby swallows first learned to sing—heavenly. Now, his only wish was to follow in the footsteps of his disciples and transform himself into a swallow, to soar high above the forest, to carry wet mud in his beak and to build a small nest among the beams and rafters...

However, Wushi's wish would never come true. One day, he tried a wild fruit brought back by Liu. At night, an excruciating pain grew in his belly. He told Liu to bury him in the pit and, after his death, cover his body with swallow droppings. Liu did as he was told.

That spring slipped away swiftly. Soon, all the azalea flowers faded, and the last swallow had left the temple. By this time, Liu had lost any desire to return home. He just sat in the main hall quietly, peace and solitude all around. The only sound was made when night fell and the bats would fly out of the hole in the walls. They sounded like bubbles bursting, breaking the long lasting silence. He no longer went out to collect wild fruit either. When hunger struck, he would simply dig the dirt and gulp it down. Gradually, he became like Wushi, stuck deep in a pit he had dug himself. He became blind too, but his hearing was now exceptionally acute. Every year when the swallows came back, he would sober up from his bewilderment and carefully capture every single sound made by them and become intoxicated. No one knows how many years passed. Liu grew old. He thought he would have the same fate as Wushi, to die and be buried in the pit. But one day, he seemed to hear words being spoken.

The voice was soft and noble: "That man has sat in the pit for a long time!" Another soft and noble voice replied: "Yes! But how interesting can it be sitting in a pit? Why doesn't he fly out and catch worms with us?" Liu's heart twitched. He turned and listened closely, wondering why people were dropping by all of a sudden. But the sound of flying swallows followed. He could tell, they were Chuntiao and Zi'er whose nest was ten steps away on the left, next to the nest of Huahong and Naxi. He continued to follow the sounds and realized that the main hall had become very busy. Words were thrown all around: some said that there were many insects by the pool of water in the east, some said that the mud on the south was the most suitable for nest building, some were scolding a youngster for flying badly, and some were uttering sweet promises to their lovers...

Liu was first filled with joy and later with sorrow. He strove to stand-up but found his feet powerless. So he stretched out both bands, trying to crawl along the wall of the pit. He wanted out but was unable to escape. Suddenly, he felt brightness in front of his eyes. He saw light radiating from above. He lifted his arm in a sharp movement, and found himself flying out of the pit and crashing into a pillar. The pain was almost unbearable, but he was ecstatic. He flapped his wings with all his strength, but quickly crashed into a wall again. He no longer cared. He fumbled his way out of the main hall, turned his tail and dashed through the green leaves. The blue sky poured in, flooding into him with an overbearing love, encompassing him...

Many years later, the Dongke Temple was rediscovered. The azalea flowers were still blooming in front of the main gate, but all the buildings had completely collapsed. Swallows moved their nests to the cliffs. When the light of the setting sun beamed down from behind the mountain, the swallows flew between the bright light and the darkness. Sometimes like a flock of fiery, blazing birds, sometimes like a school of green fish swimming freely underwater. ∎

AUTHOR'S NOTE

Ke (柯, tree stem), in Chinese, has a particular meaning. In Tang dynasty legend, a story called "A Dream of Nangke" (《南柯一梦》) revolves around a man who is chosen to marry a princess and who becomes a high-ranking official. He conquers neighboring states but eventually fails in a political struggle. In the end, he finds himself waking up from an afternoon nap under a big tree to the south of his house, and realizes everything has just been a dream. When I chose *dongke*, a big tree on the east, for the title of my story, I followed tradition and plot; the fate of the characters were already determined.

THE FLOATING TEMPLE

飘浮在空中的兰若

As Wugen[1] sat praying in the meditation quarters, he suddenly realized how empty his life was—there was no reason for him to spend more time on the cultivation of the mind.

When he was eight, he left home to become a monk. Others did this because they were forced by circumstance, wanted to escape, or they just wanted to run off to be lazy. But when Wugen left home, it was because he believed he should spend his life immersed in the careful study of Buddhism, entrust his life to the vast emptiness, and find a realm where he required nothing—that is to say, nirvana.

He searched for the path to nirvana among Buddhist principles. He read all the Buddhist scriptures he could find, both true and false. He tried to find traces of the route within everything these scriptures said, and organize them into an organic whole, finding and rejecting falseness and, in the end, relying on these true principles to take him to his objective.

---

[1] "No Roots" or "Rootless"

He found, however, all manner of contradictions in these scriptures. Maybe the route to the Buddhist kingdom would lead him instead to hell. Just as religious discipline can lead to the breaking of religious precepts, Buddhism could turn you into a demon; his long study of Chan principles found him thinking of the sweet, soft bodies of the opposite sex, whereupon he could lose himself in everyday tasks—carrying water, planting vegetables, eating, drinking, begging for alms. In the end, he gave up meditation and ceased researching Buddhist scriptures, believing that the real Buddhist principles lay in everyday life.

At thirty, he began to research Go and at thirty-five he took up musical instruments. At thirty-six he started painting and penning poems, and at thirty-seven he found an old monk to teach him martial arts. That old, taciturn monk assisted in the monastery kitchen. By the time Wugen had become a well-known, high-ranking monk; even high-ranking officials considered meeting him an honor.

At forty, Wugen returned to secular life—not formally, as his petition to do so was denied. Thus he gave up the temple and slipped away in the middle of the night, going to Jiankang city, where nobody knew him. He wore plain clothing, had short, messy hair, and spent much of his time in brothels. When he was out of money he'd steal from the wealthy or beg. He lived this way until fifty-five. He didn't think anyone would recognize him, the world forgetting the Dharma name of the once auspicious monk, Wugen.

Quite by chance, Minister Zhu Yi and Wugen both became enamored with a certain prostitute, who told Zhu Yi that among her frequent customers there was an odd man who liked to have sex with her in a meditation position. Zhu Yi was quite curious and asked the prostitute to introduce them. He left a name card, which she passed on to Wugen the next time he visited. Wugen wrote a polite letter employing complex prose and ornate calligraphy, in which he refused the invitation.

Zhu Yi, however, instantly recognized Wugen's handwriting, as he'd met him when he was a low-ranking official on a visit to Biyun Temple. Wugen had been a monk there, and had given him a poem as a memento.

Wugen's secular life thus came to an end. Because he was never officially released, it was a cut-and-dry case: the sanctimonious Minister Zhu Yi sent people to forcibly transport him back to Biyun Temple at Moling. It is believed he did so out of jealousy.

At Biyun Temple, Wugen was forced to shave his head and once again put on monk's robes, demoted to the lowest level monk and often mocked as a deserter.

But in truth, were he to escape again, no one would have stopped him; despite being fifty-five, he was still quite strong and an experienced martial artist. No one knew why Wugen didn't run away or petition to leave, but he'd lost his passion for secular life—or, rather, his lust for the opposite sex. He humbly performed the tasks of the lowest-ranking monk at Biyun Temple—emptying the latrines, watering vegetables, chopping wood, and of course attending morning and evening lessons. He seemed satisfied with his lot.

The year he turned sixty—on a morning not unlike any other—he sat in meditation with other monks when he suddenly realized the emptiness of his life—in this world, as well as other worlds, there was no reason to spend any more time in the further cultivation of the mind.

He felt a deep despair, a void which could not be filled, even with death, a notion that intensified his depression.

The monks at the temple felt a tremor. All but Wugen stood. They looked at each other and seemed to all realize that it was an earthquake. They ran, frightened, out of the meditation room and gathered in the open space in front of the main hall. The earthquake grew in intensity and the lacquered tiles fell like rain from the roof of the main hall. The stupas shook back and forth as some of the walls collapsed. The monks were scared, terrified that the end of the world had come. They cried out in fear, some reciting Buddhist chants.

Then, the earthquake stopped. The head monk ordered that a party descend the mountain to check on the situation in Moling village. Other monks gathered food and water and some went to retrieve mats and blankets as they planned to sleep outdoors that night and observe the situation. Just as these monks were busying themselves, those few who had been sent down to Moling village returned. The head monk was quite surprised by their swift return—as well as the odd expressions on their faces.

"Master, we're flying!" a monk yell as he ran in through the outer gate.

Another monk yelled, "Master, there was no earthquake! But we can't get off the mountain!"

Another monk, a bit calmer than the others, entered the gate last, saying to the head monk: "Master, the mountain is flying!"

The head monk walked out of the gate and from there, through the thick pine forest, he could see Moling village, shrouded in mist. He could feel the mountain slowly rising. The calmest monk walked over to him and said: "Master, we went to the foot of the mountain, but there's no way to get down, because the mountain's already dozens of meters off the ground.

The head monk had all the monks temporarily stop work and return to the area in front of the main hall; he took the monks who had already been back down the mountain with him.

Biyun Temple was situated on Mount Wu, five kilometers away from Moling village. By the time the head monk walked down the mountain path to the edge of the forest, Mount Wu had ceased ascending and was already about fifty meters off the ground.

Upon seeing the flying mountain, the residents of Moling flooded from the village, with only the infirm and some children left behind. Seeing a mountain suspended in the air, they took this as an omen that the Buddha would return. They carried incense sticks and sacrificial items and placed them below Mount Wu, and the head official ordered the local squires to kowtow in front of the incense.

Mount Wu neither rose nor lowered. It just floated in the air like a giant mirage.

The monks of Biyun Temple tried to get the mountain back to the ground. First, they put on their robes, arranged incense, flowers, and fruits, and knelt in front of the Buddhist statues, begging the Buddha to save them, to free them from their predicament, but their prostrations and prayers had no effect. The white clouds moved slowly in the clear sky, casting shadows that glided across Moling village past the wild fields outside, over Mount Wu and Biyun Temple, dozens of meters in the sky, and then back over the fields outside of Moling village.

The curious villagers gradually dispersed, and only a few remained—those with family at the temple, the officials designated responsible, and people with nothing better to do. By the afternoon, the head monk had given up on prayers and decided to lower a few people down by rope. The monks found sixty meters of hemp rope and tied one end around a pine tree and the other around the waist of a volunteer.

The volunteer was lowered toward the surface, but never seemed to get any closer to the ground. Mount Wu seemed to rise. Worried that the mountain would rise too high for the rope, he yelled out to be lowered more quickly, but the rate of the mountain's rise and his rate of descent were the same. When they were out of rope, the mountain stopped rising, but there were still dozens of meters between him and the ground. The monks had no choice but to pull him back up, but the mountain didn't lower itself in response; it stayed at the same height. By this time, they were more than a hundred meters off the ground. If one climbed to the top of the highest stupa at Biyun Temple, they could see the Yangtze River like a silk cord floating upon the earth. None of the monks discovered this, and even if they had, they wouldn't have been in the mood to appreciate it.

With the grain and vegetables stored in the temple, the monks didn't have any pressing survival issues to worry about. After the sun set, the monks returned to the temple to eat and conducted their evening studies as normal, with nothing said throughout the night.

On the morning of the second day, a number of people from Moling village tried to make a new hill under the mountain, hoping to be able to reach Mount Wu and bring the monks down. They dug a hole by the large pit left by the mountain, and began piling up dirt, but they quickly discovered that their efforts were in vain, as the higher they piled the dirt, the higher the mountain rose. They gave up this venture and, in the following days, they tried scaling ladders and siege engines, but these approaches also led the mountain to rise.

They did, however, discover a way to communicate: arrows. They could shoot arrows from the surface to Mount Wu, and it was easy for those on the mountain to simply drop messages back. This also demonstrated that the monks were perfectly capable of returning to the surface, but the journey would be paid for with their lives.

The monks within the temple became increasingly depressed. Even though they had sufficient vegetables and grain, and could solve long-term problems by bringing more land under cultivation, they tended toward despair as they were cut off from the world—a world they could see all too easily. One day, they discovered that the well had run dry and despair turned to panic; thankfully, the head monk ordered the digging of deep pits at four locations around the mountain. They were lined with stones from the compound wall (for which they already had no use), and they were able to collect rainwater for the few dozen monks at the temple, enough to scrape by.

Things got worse and worse, however, as sadness and despair grew. Morning and night classes were no longer held regularly, and even though the head monk and those with strong beliefs held on, there were a few monks who ceased their studies, and some who even caught birds in the forest to eat.

Finally, one day, a monk jumped from the mountain. Even though everyone was certain that this would happen eventually, when it actually did, they were shocked. They could see the monk's body on the surface below, his fresh blood dyeing the green grass bright red.

The people of Moling village had almost forgotten the monks. Every month the head official sent archers to deliver a message of goings-on in the village and a few comforting words. That was all. Of course, there wasn't much more to say or do—no way to deliver food or water. Besides a little emotional support, what else could be done?

This isn't to say that Mount Wu was abandoned. In fact, a constant stream of travelers came to see the miracle of Mount Wu. Writers and poets penned tributes to memorialize the event. These were carved on steles and set in front of the giant pit, which by now was a lake. "Mount Wu of the Thunder and Rain" had become a famous scenic spot. When the rain fell heavily, a huge curtain of water would stream down from Mount Wu and flutter like a white veil in the wind.

After three monks had committed suicide, the head monk decided to close the temple gate, and forbade the monks from venturing out alone. He also forced the monks to participate in morning and night classes and observe religious discipline. Cultivation of new vegetable patches and the raising of fruit and grain began, participation in which was compulsory. Slowly, the head monk discovered, the monks shed their sadness and despair. Reading scripture, observing discipline, and working hard allowed them to forget their situation.

No more suicides occurred, and the monks seemed happy and calm. The gate was reopened, and the monks regained freedom of movement.

At this time, Wugen died. Only then did the other monks even remember that he was there. They reflected and realized that he'd been unusually calm throughout the entire ordeal, that seemingly nothing attracted his attention. He went about as normal cleaning latrines, watering vegetables, chopping wood, and reading scripture. Thus, he was forgotten, and the monks buried him in the cemetery behind the temple, and a small stone stele was put upon his grave which read: "Here Lies Sakyamuni Wugen."

Emperor Wu of Liang, Xiao Yan, took with him a number of eunuchs, palace maids, and military officials from Jiankang to Moling village to observe the miracle of Biyun Temple and offer incense. The magistrate of Moling village notified the temple's head monk ten days in advance. On the morning of that day, all the still-living monks of the temple arranged their clothes neatly and came to the foot of the mountain to await the arrival of the emperor and officials. Xiao Yan communicated with the monks through a eunuch with good lungs and a loud voice.

"To...the...monks...up...above...I...send...my...regards, I am... the...emperor, I am...here to... visit...you," the eunuch yelled loudly, and Xiao Yan smiled as he waved at the monks.

The monks knelt on the ground, and a young monk also with a loud vocal capacity did his part, yelling: "Emperor...we are...honored! Thank you...for your...good wishes! We are...doing...fine...on the mountain! " Yelling back and forth, their necks throbbed, and their faces turned red.

After a few rounds of pleasantries, the emperor ordered his personal guard to bind some incense to their arrows and fire it upward. The monks burned the incense for the emperor, and then the court painter produced a painting of the emperor and his officials with the mountain behind them. After that, a number of painters came to Mount Wu to provide this service to travelers, at a price of about 1,000 copper coins per painting. It wasn't cheap, but they still did great business.

Xiao Yan encountered trouble not long after he returned to Jiankang. One of his generals, Hou Jing, betrayed him and dispatched soldiers to seize him. The traitors besieged him and the crown prince, and Xiao Yan's formerly loyal supporters fell into a spiral of scheming and infighting. Although a large number of troops still supported him, they were unable to break the siege.

The magistrate of Moling had been recently assigned—his predecessor was promoted and transferred to the capital because of his successful reception of the emperor, and was trapped inside the city by the rebellion. But the monthly letter of communication to Biyun Temple was the same as always. The head monk held a ceremony of the highest order to pray for the emperor. However, their prayers were in vain as the emperor and the crown prince remained trapped until winter.

In a letter from the magistrate to the temple, it was mentioned that one of the crown prince's carpenters had built a giant kite, and attached to it an imperial script, sending it flying in the hopes that it would reach the troops loyal to him and that they would come to save him. However, the plan failed as the kite was shot down by Hou Jing's troops as it passed over their territory. This letter gave an idea to the head monk: He remembered that they had access to a bamboo forest, which would give them material to build gliders. Thus, he ordered the monks to chop down the bamboo and cut it into strips. The monks were enthused by the entire plan, as it meant they'd have a chance to return to the surface, a hope which they had long since abandoned.

It wasn't long until the first glider was completed. The monks made wings out of Buddhist scriptures. The head monk was initially unwilling to agree to this use of the scripture, as cloth was a better choice and they had a small supply of both. However, without cloth, the monks wouldn't survive the winter, so in the end the head monk was left with no choice but to agree to the use the pages from their books to construct the wings. As the glider had to carry a human, it had to be quite large.

The monks were careful in their construction, releasing the glider from the top of the stupas to see if it could descend stably. As they had no experience in the construction of such devices, their first attempt failed. The construction more or less toppled to the ground, the frame was destroyed, and the paper ripped. On their next attempt, they made smaller test models to save time and resources, producing small gliders that could land reliably before they started work on a newer, large model. They wrote of their work in a letter to tell the magistrate of Moling. They had previously delivered their letters to him by affixing them to a rock and simply dropping it, but this time they attached it to a small gliding kite, and hung a rock from the bottom. When they set off the glider, it flew off, and even with the stone attached, it maintained equilibrium. It arrived successfully in the hands of the magistrate's runner, and the monks cheered with hope and excitement at their initial success.

The magistrate sent them diagrams made by a skilled kite-maker in a letter, and the monks made a new large glider in accordance with these instructions. It flew down from the stupa quite successfully, and almost off the mountain. Luckily, the monks were able to catch the glider (and the precious materials) before that happened.

For the next test, they prepared to attach a person.

The first test subject was decided by drawing lots, but the head monk, determined to be the last to leave, did not participate in this trial run. The test was successful, and the glider with the man attached flew down from the highest peak to Mount Wu's pine forest. The branches of the pine trees broke the paper in a few places, but the monk was unharmed.

The damage to the wings was repaired, and the head monk wrote the time of the planned flight in a letter which was sent to the magistrate's runner: noon, five days hence. Soon the whole village was abuzz with the news. However, when the day finally came, high winds kicked up, and even though the villagers gathered under the mountain to see the first monk return to the surface, the head monk chose to delay the flight. After all, after so much time, what was two more days? There was no reason to add unnecessary risks.

The chosen monk's heart was full of joy and trepidation. He wanted to return to the surface and be with his family, but worried about his safety. His name had been transmitted in a letter; at this point letters were exchanged more than once a day.

On the appointed day, the pilot monk's parents came

early to the area below the mountain, and the magistrate of Moling arrived around ten on an ox-driven cart. The weather was clear, and there was only a light wind, nothing to prevent the test of a return flight to the surface. The monk was bound firmly to the frame of the glider, and a large area of forest had been cleared to give him a runway. It was a moving sight.

The monk jumped into the clear blue sky, and the glider coasted stably. Just as people began to cheer, the paper wing ripped and the craft lost all stability. Flipping over and over in mid-air, it took a straight dive down. The crowd was transfixed by the tragedy. He didn't die immediately. Perhaps he had some small comfort in his final moments by being taken in his mother's arms.

It was clear that paper wasn't reliable enough. It had to be cloth. The monks tore down the curtains in the main hall and cut up their clothes for the summer, then their mosquito nets. Besides, it was winter; there were no mosquitoes anyway. They made a few large gliders and tested each of them on the stupas. This time, they didn't draw lots to see who went, electing to have the eldest fly first and the youngest last. The head monk still insisted on being the very last to fly.

As the monks scrambled to make gliders, the people of Moling observed a shift in the position and height of the mountain—it had moved closer to the village but floated higher. Although the change was slow, after a number of days it became quite clear. The magistrate of the village notified the head monk of this fact in a letter, but the head monk didn't tell the others as to not incite panic. One night there was a strong northwesterly wind, and the monks noticed that the mountain was swaying. In the morning, when some went to sweep leaves, they were startled to see that they were already quite close to the village and that the mountain's height had increased by a third. Contrary to the head monk's expectations, they were all quite calm at learning this and they simply increased the speed at which they worked. The higher the mountain rose, the greater the danger of descent. If the mountain came to rest over the village, then the monks might not be able to find a safe landing spot.

The flight times for the second batch of five monks were decided. They were to fly two days earlier than they planned. When the day arrived, even though the weather wasn't great, the head monk decided to go ahead. When the oldest monk was bound to his glider, he changed his mind at the last second and decided that he wouldn't go back, wishing to remain on Mount Wu. Even though the mountain might be blown by the wind over the sea, he was unwilling to leave. The head monk tried to persuade him, but his conviction was strong. The old monk had no family on the surface, so in the end, the head monk agreed, and the next oldest monk was bumped up in the order.

One by one, the monks went down. They succeeded.

All five of the monks survived, with one breaking a leg and one landing in the water and almost drowning, but he was thankfully rescued by the many observers on the surface.

The next round of gliders used the robes of the five departed monks and the fifteen about to go, as well as a number of mats. The monks picked up the pace, first because they were more experienced now, and second because they were worried about another north-westerly wind coming to blow them higher. They pulled together and assembled the next fifteen gliders in just a few days' time. They conducted only the most basic safety tests, and didn't run stability checks from the stupas. Almost all the monks from this round made it to the ground safely, with only a few sustaining light injuries. The residents of Moling village cheered with each arrival, and the news spread through the country, with even the usurper Hou Jing, newly established as the emperor of his own state, sending a messenger bearing congratulations for the monks' bravery and wisdom.

Two days after the second round of fifteen monks returned, a strong northwesterly wind rose. The temperature dropped sharply, and snow fell during the night. Only fifteen monks remained on the mountain, and the head monk heard them crying at night.

In the morning, as they feared, Mount Wu was over Moling village. It was at least two hundred meters in the air.

Looking down from this height, there was a wide panoramic view of the village. The monks had to decide whether to quickly return to the surface or wait for the mountain to drift further. In the end, they elected to return immediately. Even if they might find better landing spots after passing the village, the mountain would definitely rise even higher. They weren't willing to take that risk.

The third round of gliders was also completed quickly. They used up the last of the materials, and, as they were quite a lot higher off the ground, the gliders were made at a large scale. However, when they finished the fourteenth glider, they suddenly realized that they were almost out of bamboo, with only a small amount remaining, just enough to make a very small glider, smaller even than the second round. Even though there was the one old monk unwilling to return to the surface, this meant that one of the monks would have to ride the small craft down. The head monk reassured the others, and told them he would take the runt, seeing as he was the thinnest of all the monks at the monastery.

The monks had nothing left to do except to wait for the next northwesterly wind to come. They were already quite clear on the fact that they could use wind to take them to the outskirts of the village and that at the same time wind could add to their gliding distance and thus their vertical speed with respect to their descent. They prayed that a northwesterly wind would not come in the night. The head monk told the magistrate of the village in a letter about the plans for the last round of monks; by this point the communication was one-way, as nobody was strong enough to shoot an arrow to that height.

The wind rose very early in the morning, at which time the monks bound each other to the gliders and clasped their hands as a gesture of farewell to the old monk unwilling to leave. They, one after another, shakily ascended the highest stupa and waited for dawn.

The sun rose over the horizon, looking very small, wavering in the wind like the surface's beating heart. One monk exited the stupa and climbed to the corner of the rafters, exerting great efforts to stay stable. A monk inside the structure held his hand to keep him from drifting away before he was ready. In order to use the element, the monk turned his back to the sun, his entire glider facing the wind. He nodded his head, and the other monk released his grip. He flew off swiftly, and for a second seemed to almost fly upwards, but quickly swooped down. The other monks watched him rapidly disappear into the darkness of the dawn.

The monks walked out of the stupa one after another and drifted toward the surface, the last being the head monk. The residents of Moling village hadn't slept the previous night. On hearing the unbridled cries of the wind, they knew it was the time for the monks to return. They gathered in the square in front of the magistrate's office, heads raised, looking at Mount Wu hanging heavily in the windy dark sky, almost invisible.

Just as dawn turned to sunrise, the white of a fish's belly revealing itself over the black line of the horizon, the people saw a small black dot float down from the distant Mount Wu. A group of already prepared young people took off in the direction of the small black dot, running at full speed out of the settlement. They all counted down, knowing there were fourteen monks flying, with the head monk going last and the fifteenth opting to stay. Thirteen had already arrived, with the fourteenth small flier still nowhere to be seen. People began to become uneasy, worrying that the head monk wouldn't return.

At this time, a fire broke out on Mount Wu, and Biyun Temple began to burn. Just as people began to despair, the small black dot appeared. It was so small, so light. Everyone cheered.

The sun had fully risen by this point. Mount Wu floated past the city, and most of the residents of the village followed it on the ground, walking out of the village. The mountain looked tiny by then, and the black dot was tinier still. People raised their heads and strained to see, trying to determine the direction where the little dot would fly. But he seemed to rise higher and higher—perhaps the wind had picked up, perhaps he was just too light. Either way, the black dot didn't descend. He was blown up and up by the north westerlywind, higher and higher, as if he was ascending to the sun. Maybe he would land in the sea, or maybe somewhere beyond the sea.

Reports came in of the monks being found, thirteen in total. Three had died upon landing, and the others had varying degrees of injuries. Except, of course, for the head monk—who simply floated away, last seen more than five kilometers outside of the city.

The residents of Moling dispatched ten young people to the east to search for the head monk. They traveled and searched all the way to the ocean, but found nothing. ∎

AUTHOR'S NOTE

Between the age twenty and thirty, I wanted to write fiction, but didn't know what to write. "Pure literature" and rural literature were the fashion of the time. One day, I accidentally discovered a whole set of the *Extensive Records of the Taiping Era* (《太平广记》)on the very top of a bookshelf in the library, which no one had touched in the past decade. I took it home and read it without missing a single word. I finally discovered that my mother tongue was traditional Chinese culture...I started to write in the style of Tang dynasty fantasy, but I knew it wasn't a simple process of copying. I am not worried about resembling the ancients, because I am a modern man of distinctive thoughts. I write what I find interesting and naturally formed the style you see.

TAGEXING 踏歌行

Tagexing is a brand manager for a Fortune 500 company by day and novelist and screenwriter by night. A signed writer with the Xuanwuji Writing Team (玄武纪写作小组), a group of aspiring young authors mentored by seasoned *wuxia* writers, she has published various stories in installments in Modern and Ancient Legends, Wuxia Edition (《今古传奇·武侠版》), one of the most popular *wuxia* magazines in China. She's currently working on a screenplay adapted from the novel series *Jianke* (《键客》). Follow her on Sina Weibo @踏歌行-玄武纪.

BOW

弓

"Branches, horns, tendons, glue, thread, and paint—all these things must be harvested in the proper season," he said, carving a strip of mulberry wood he was working. "Once the six materials are prepared, the craftsman must work delicately to fashion a bow. The branch should be retrieved in the winter, the horn in the spring, and tendon in the summer. The other materials should be obtained in the fall. The bow must be fashioned in winter and then checked again at the next cold to see if the varnish has cracked[1]. All in all, the process takes three or four years..."

I lay off to the side on a wooden cart he had made, covered with wooden strips and bandages all over my body, unable to move. The sky was getting dark, and as the wind blew, it brought with it the chill of imminent snow.

He was my master, a wizened, thin old craftsman crippled in one leg. Ten days prior, I had been beaten and severely injured, my feet and hands broken. There was

---

[1] From *Rites of Zhou* (《周礼》), a record of politics, economy, culture, customs, rituals, and laws of the states from the pre-Qin period (before 221 BCE)

nowhere on my body that was intact. He happened to be at my home to deliver some farming tools he'd fixed when he saw the ruined state I was in. He asked to take me on as his apprentice for some reason, but my parents were opposed. I managed to whisper my acceptance, however, and followed him out.

I couldn't stand that house any longer.

"Stay still, but keep your mind moving!" He saw me drifting off, but continued coolly. "This bow is going to be of your making!"

"Heh," I laughed. I wanted to mock him but couldn't come up with a response, so I let it drop.

This wasn't real. I didn't want to be a bow-maker. But, with this old man's help, I could heal properly. I could kill Shi Meng and avenge my sister.

It was the second year of the reign of King Jian of Qi, and I was fourteen years old. Our home was in a small mountain village near Jimo in the state of Qi. Although we were poor, we got by. If my sister hadn't been accosted by Shi Meng on the way back from delivering some tools for repair, we could have continued living peacefully.

I remembered how warm the sunlight was that day. After I finished helping my parents with tasks on the farm, I went to meet my sister on her way back and happened to see Shi Meng and a dozen or so others forcing her into an alleyway.

I'm not very tall, and could only see white skin and red blood between the gathered people. I went forward to save her but was blocked by four or five people, like a caged chicken. I cried loudly, and was beaten by them severely, with filthy rags stuffed into my mouth.

When I returned home, my parents alternated between scolding and soothing me. My sister didn't receive that kind of treatment. She spent three days locked in her room crying, unable to come out.

I wanted to go in to keep her company, but my parents wouldn't let me, telling me I didn't understand the gravity of the situation and that I could have gotten myself killed. To my parents, what was a daughter? After being sullied, she was basically unfit for marriage, but if an old widower were to come by looking for a wife, they would give her to him without a second thought.

As for me, Shao Yun, I was the precious only son.

Ten days ago, on the night of the first heavy snow, my sister used a hemp rope and quietly hanged herself in her room.

As my parents gathered up her corpse, I took an axe and went looking for Shi Meng at his house. For this I was beaten almost to death by Shi Meng's thugs, my limbs broken. It's odd when I think how, after these incidents, our neighbors avoided us, afraid of any kind of conflict with Shi Meng. And yet this craftsman who subsisted on making farming tools took me in as his own, cared for me with all his heart, and thought he could make me his apprentice.

"It's cold, go inside." When I showed no reaction, he grew cross. "Someone will be here soon, go in and don't make any noise."

When he finished speaking, he remembered I could not move. He sighed, and gathered up the materials around him, preparing to push me inside.

I heard the sound of footsteps outside the courtyard.

It wasn't one person; it was a group. They clamored and brought with them a noxious air.

I knew who it was.

I was a boy of fourteen with the audacity to show up at Shi Meng's door with an axe—a serious affront to his mighty thug reputation—how could he not respond in force?

The cart was heavy, and my master pushed me all the way inside when the wooden door was forcefully shoved open. Shi Meng sauntered in, a blade of grass in his mouth, eyes full of malice.

"Little cripple, here you are!" He took a step forward, arms crossed, as the dozen or so thugs behind him flooded in to fill the courtyard.

My master stopped and turned toward Shi Meng and the others, bowing with his hands folded in front of him in a show of respect. "Shao Yun is my new disciple. His parents entrusted his care to me, so please do not affront my honor."

As soon as he finished speaking, the assembled thugs broke into peals of laughter.

"I wouldn't have thought an old cripple would be so plucky!" Shi Meng wiped his nose as he walked forward. "Now I see how you lost the use of your leg." As he moved, the other thugs followed, making a move to flank us.

I clenched my fists as my heart beat like a drumroll.

I didn't know my master well at all. How could I let such an innocent get involved? But what could I do?

"Don't worry." My master remained calm and smiled at Shi Meng. "I prepared a little something; maybe I can give it to Mr. Shi for his trouble."

"Oh?" Shi Meng raised his eyebrows.

Master stepped sideways into the workshop and re-emerged with a pitch-black object.

Upon seeing the object, Shi Meng exclaimed: "An iron sword! You can make weapons!" He hurriedly pulled the sword from its scabbard, his face full of surprise.

Such iron implements were extremely rare in civilian hands. The normal tools my master produced were of average quality—who would have thought that he could make something like this?

Shi Meng beheld the cold, beautiful blade, almost unable to take it in.

"I studied Moism[2]." My master spoke first, patting his

---

[2] A school of thought that evolved at the same time of Confucianism. Its best-known belief is "impartial care." Moists also emphasize the study of physical science and mathematics and were regarded as great engineers, often hired by states in warfare.

lame leg. He smiled, face full of wrinkles. "I did something I shouldn't have when I was young. If Mr. Shi can keep it quiet, I'd be more than willing to fashion you some fine weapons."

As I heard that, my blood froze. How could he do that?

"All right!" Shi Meng's eyes sparkled as he sheathed his weapon. "With things as they are, I think we have an agreement." He walked slowly over and sneered as he looked at me. "My quarrel with your disciple is finished. It wasn't a big deal."

As I looked in his eyes, I could feel my own teeth grinding audibly.

"Also, recently I've been studying under the sword master Changchui from the school of the Eastern Dragon. You know, even if he had a problem, it's nothing to me." He saw the hatred in my eyes, and spoke purposefully.

"Shi Meng! You..." I growled angrily, but my master put his hand over my mouth. The smell of wax on his hand was nauseating.

"Ha!" Shi Meng said cheerfully. "Then I'll entrust the provision of weapons for my brothers to you." He paused briefly. "Also, I hear that business in weapons is quite good. Would you, master, have any interest in taking up your old trade?"

"Shao Yun! Don't move!"

I was carrying my belongings on my back as I

walked out with the aid of crutches—but I had been discovered. He carried a bowl of medicinal soup as he limped after me, making it to the gate where he breathed heavily, glaring at me. "You already accepted me as your master, you must stay and learn!"

"Learn what? Bow-making?" I chuckled. "For my enemies who killed my sister?"

Close up, I took a good look at my master for the first time.

His clothes were filthy. His face was covered in deep wrinkles, and he smelled of a bitter scent all over. His thin, unkempt hair was bound at the back of his head like a bundle of straw.

He looked different now, his eyes burning with a hot light, as if they were trying to tell me something. More importantly, I noticed that, as he'd come running out, the bowl of soup in his hand, full to the brim, was completely still, without of even any ripples. Not a drop had spilled.

"You..." I was too shocked to say anything.

He gave me the bowl of soup. "I'll teach you how to make bows and how to use them."

I really had never had any indication that my master understood martial arts. He was just a crippled old man living in a town in the middle of nowhere, unable to even lift a blade. But there was a great deal he could teach me, though at the time, I wasn't ready to learn.

Shi Meng had begun studying under a great sword master and had acquired a fine new sword. A fierce fighter with training—how could I hope to ever face him?

I didn't accept that bowl of soup. I threw down my bundle and my crutches, bearing the pain of my unmended bones, knelt in snow before my master, and touched my head to the ground three times.

"Please, master, get rid of Shi Meng and for the rest of my life I will obey all your orders and carry on the traditions of the House of Mo!"

He became suddenly furious and poured the bowl of scalding soup all over my head.

"Your vengeance is your own business!" He threw the bowl to the ground, shattering it, and took off in a huff. "I just want to make a legendary bow! If you're not interested, then leave!"

Of course, I didn't leave. From then on, I couldn't be kept away from the studio.

How else could I get revenge on those who killed my sister and live to see it?

The first year, I hadn't fully healed. I spent my time learning the basics of martial arts and how to make bows.

"Branches, horns, tendons, glue, thread, and paint—all these things must be harvested in the proper season." My master started to teach me from the beginning. "Once the six materials are prepared, the craftsman must work delicately to fashion a bow."

The second year, I'd fully recovered, and my master began to teach me how to build up strength in my arms. The injuries to the bone meant that my arms shook violently, and it was hard for me to even hold chopsticks. My master made painstaking efforts to reset the broken tendons in my arms.

Shi Meng found a channel for selling the weapons, so we moved out of the small workshop and into a large new house.

The third year, I started formally training in martial arts. I was seventeen. My body grew quickly, and I started to grow facial hair.

That was when the bow in my hand started to take shape, a grayish, yellow bow that began to shine when it was polished. When covered with black varnish, it took on a dignified, austere look. The bowstring was firm and hard, imparting a slight curve to the bow stem. It was a strong long-distance bow, one that could easily pierce leather armor. If fired up close, it could run through the human body.

I knew my time for vengeance was coming.

In the middle of the fourth year, Shi Meng made a large business deal. The state of Zhao suffered a crushing defeat and saw its supplies scattered, meaning they were urgently in need of replacements. My master happily accepted the order without hesitation. With that order completed, my master would be set for life.

My archery had improved, and the poplars in the courtyard were full of holes from my arrows, like so many tiny eyes. However, my master never praised me and refused to give me a precise appraisal of my skills.

According to him, until you had taken a life, you didn't truly understand the meaning of war.

I didn't think so. Why would I have to kill someone to test my mettle? How would I be any different from Shi Meng?

To my surprise, my master took his ox out of its pen—the first thing he'd bought when he arrived in this town. Even though he didn't need to plough the fields, he looked upon the animal as his companion and cared for it fondly.

My master tied the ox to a poplar and told me to kill it with one shot. He then turned and left.

Looking at that old animal, I saw it gaze upon my master's retreating figure—it seemed to know something was amiss. I could see the pain in its eyes. This was new.

I slowly drew back the bowstring. It had never felt this hard before, like it was cutting into my fingers.

The tip of the arrow quivered as it pointed at the ox's head.

I closed my eyes, gritted my teeth, and loosed the arrow.

A dull thud sounded out, and my body trembled as I accidently bit my tongue. It hurt.

"Done." My master walked up with his hands clasped behind his back.

The arrow had passed straight through the ox's head, heart, and tail.

The setting sun was crimson like the ox's blood. I looked over at my master as he bent down to hold the ox's body, a flash of light in his eye.

I was ready. In four years' time, Shi Meng's swordsmanship had also improved considerably, and he had under his command far more than just those couple of thugs. He was now the head of an army of brigands almost a hundred strong, serving as mercenaries for other states. They had the appearance of merchants, and with weapons in their hands, they went about causing chaos, killing, robbing, and plundering.

I was scared and somewhat blamed my master. If he hadn't taken up this weapon business, Shi Meng wouldn't have become the powerful menace that he was.

One day, I was delivering a diagram to Shi Meng's compound and saw him kill someone.

It was a young knight—tall, handsome, and dignified. His blade was two-and-a-half feet long, black inlaid with gold, shining like a slippery snake that refused to be confined.

The knight had come to Shi Meng to seek justice for a

widowed mother and her baby. Shi Meng was looking for a private channel to move his cargo and had flattened a farmer who was blocking his way.

The young knight brought only one blade without a scabbard. I hid in a corner of the courtyard and watch wide-eyed as Shi Meng had his underlings surround the young man and take turns going at him until his blood covered the floor of the courtyard.

Then, Shi Meng came down, drew his sword, first cut off his right arm, then his left arm, then his right leg, then his left leg, and finally his head.

After leaving Shi Meng's mansion, I didn't go back to the workshop. I went home.

I hadn't been home for four years. When my parents went to the workshop to see me, I never received them. I hated them for what they did to my sister. My bones would ache, and I'd have trouble sleeping at night.

I had to see them after I'd delivered the diagram, and I'd managed to sneak off with the knight's head without Shi Meng noticing.

My parents' hair had turned white with time, and the house had changed considerably. My sister's room had been leveled and turned into a small vegetable patch.

I found a shovel, dug up an area, and buried the head inside.

I didn't know his name, so I couldn't set up a tombstone.

My parents almost fainted with fear, but I didn't want to explain the situation.

Afterward, I took everything of value in the home, wrapped it up into a few bundles and pushed my parents out onto the street. I told them to go anywhere, as long as they didn't come back—ever.

This was the start of my war with Shi Meng.

On my way back to the workshop, I changed clothes and continued to polish my bow.

I didn't tell my master about what happened because, as the weapons business grew, I was less and less able to gauge his perspective. He was, after all, my master. If he sided with Shi Meng, I wouldn't be able to take revenge.

Life was stable and peaceful now, and Shi Meng had been decent to me. What would an insignificant old score mean to my master?

However, the bow...

The bow was complete. There was nothing stopping me.

Finally, on the day of the first heavy snow, Shi Meng came.

He was coming to collect product and I went to open the gate, pretending all was normal, and as I did, two bloody heads rolled out. Rage gripped me, my eyes nearly ruptured with fury.

My parents!

Shi Meng stood cross-armed with his sword outside the gate with a fake smile. Around him, forty or fifty thugs with weapons raised came charging.

"Brat, I didn't think that your master was so talented. He taught you how to hide well!"

I picked up my parents' heads, and took a few steps back. I'd underestimated him!

I expected that he might have noticed the head missing—maybe torturing or kidnapping my family as recompense—but I never thought the he would have seen me hiding.

My parents' blood was already cold, but against my chest, it felt like fire.

But my bow was not at my side.

I'd hidden it in the highest rafters, planning to snipe Shi Meng as he exited the warehouse after checking the product with my master.

There was no hope of that.

The fifty or so brigands flooded in, surrounding me. I clutched the two heads, with nowhere to go.

"Oh Master Cui, Master Cui Nan!" Shi Meng yelled towards the workshop. "Your disciple is about to die here today! Why don't you come out and tell him why?"

A crack of thunder exploded over my head.

My master had sold me out.

I looked at Shi Meng. Through a slight gap in his collar, I could see an ugly Adam's apple.

"I wouldn't have thought this old cripple would turn out to be Master Cui, the mighty Dark Sword Cui Nan!"

He spoke deliberately, with hatred, eyes fixed upon the courtyard gate, waiting for the form of my master to come hobbling out.

I suddenly felt something was amiss—Shi Meng's hatred of my master greatly exceeded his hatred of me.

"Cui Nan? Please," I said with disdain. "He's just a greedy old man, afraid to die."

Shi Meng turned around suddenly, face full of hatred as he came at me. "You still want to pretend! You guys make a good pair! The last batch of products I delivered fell apart as soon as I handed it over to the client! You ruined in one night the business I spent four years building!" The veins on his forehead bulged as he drew his sword.

A forceful voice sounded out: "Don't forget, I forged your sword, too!"

I quickly lifted my head.

A black form came whirling down from the eaves covered in snow.

"Shao Yun, get your bow!"

EPILOGUE

I crouched in the snow, covered in wounds, having almost bled out.

There were dead people all around me—my master was one of them. He was right next to me, sword extended. Hot air rose from the wounds on his shoulder.

I had one arrow left. Across from me, Shi Meng rolled up his sleeves, preparing to come at me.

I laughed coldly as I slowly drew my bowstring. The bow made a slight creaking sound, right next to my ear. It sounded like spring thunder.

I suddenly understood why my master didn't take revenge for me all those years ago.

He said he just wanted to make a bow—a legendary bow. The bow was me.

Snow fell heavily all around, in clumps. I drew the bow until it sung in the breeze.

Ha, Shi Meng. ■

AUTHOR'S NOTE

The Warring States period (475 – 221 BCE) of China was a fascinating time. Though long-lasting warfare and conflicts brought immense suffering, it was also a time when a hundred schools of thought competed with one another. States strived to reform and prosper. Philosophy, literature, military, and trade all reached certain peaks. In my story, the description on bow-making is taken from the "Office of Winter" chapter from the *Rites of Zhou*. It wasn't just about the production, but also what it takes for a weak boy to become a man with strength. Revenge is a dish best served cold, and growth requires patience. The master wouldn't avenge his disciple because he wanted to sustain the drive for him to become stronger and be his own salvation.

BOW
Illustration
by Zhou Xiaoyi [周晓毅]

WANG SHUO 王说

Wang Shuo (@Ezreal-500金) is a "Big V" opinion leader on Weibo whose identity is verified by the microblog platform and given VIP status. With over 750,000 followers, Wang writes short stories, mostly romance parodies, and published an anthology, *Bedtime Stories* (《睡前故事》), in 2016.

A LIFE IN THE DAY

一个被家暴女人的一天

0

Mrs. HE had been abused. She sat in the park, phone in hand, scrolling through the calendar.

The weather was unbelievably good, the grass as green as could be.

1

Mrs. Huang walked by her.

Huang: Oh dear!

She knew what went on in her neighbor's home. She took out a fine silk scarf, and wiped the blood from HE's face. "He hit you again? What happened?"

HE: I don't know. He went crazy over nothing.

Huang: There's always a reason. Otherwise, why would he hit you?

Huang continued: When my husband goes off, I just go along with him. It's not easy for men working out there. When they come home to let off some steam, just ignore them. Finish your own chores, so there's nothing for him to take issue with. My household is peaceful and democratic; we don't encourage violence.

HE's wound hurt, and she didn't feel like answering. She left to go find her own friends.

On the way she saw a car accident. The driver was busy on his phone, calling in favors from his connections, as a sanitation worker bled out under the wheels of the car.

2

Mrs. HE saw Wenzhu, and tears poured down her face.

HE: Wenzhu, I'm so scared. Saisheng beat me again. Me being hurt is one thing, but he let Pearl watch. Pearl was so scared that she cried.

Wenzhu: He's crazy!

HE: I want to get a divorce.

Wenzhu: That wouldn't be good for you. You don't have a job; if you leave, he'll probably get custody of Pearl.

HE: I have just cause; would I still lose my own daughter?

Wenzhu: You have just cause, he has money.

HE: He works to earn money, but I work so hard at home, so shouldn't I get a portion of our assets?

Wenzhu: There's no law that says so.

HE was pained.

HE: We just do different jobs, but my work doesn't count? Housework isn't economic activity, only profit counts? This isn't what we learned in school.

Wenzhu felt bad for her friend. They'd both been educated well and found good jobs. But the burden of keeping a house and raising her daughter was too great, and she had to quit. After that, her husband looked down on her.

3

HE's mother heard, and called.

Mother: Saisheng says you haven't been home all day. Where'd you go?

HE could only cry.

HE's mother sighed. She knew how things were with her daughter.

Mother: There will always be conflicts between husbands and wives. You just have to give and take a little, and things will clear up.

HE: I want a divorce.

Mother: You're old, who else would want you? What will your daughter do? Dear little Pearl! As a mother, how can you stand it?

HE: I'm afraid.

Mother: Women are weak by nature, but as a mother, you must be strong. Hang in there and you can get past anything.

Mrs. HE had nothing to say.

Her mother asked carefully: Did...you wrong Saisheng in any way?

HE was baffled.

Mother: I was just asking. If you didn't, that's good.

HE hung up the phone, and switched to her calendar, scrolling through it aimlessly.

4

The sky was slowly getting darker. Mrs. HE didn't dare go home. She'd left in a hurry, and hadn't brought her wallet or keys. The complex had a resident council; she could go there to try her luck.

She hadn't gone far when she saw a group of women in the courtyard, drinking tea and cracking sunflower seeds.

Woman A: In Building E5, he beat her up again.

Woman B: Oh no... what did she do?

Woman A: No idea.

Woman B: Mrs. HE is quite good-looking, and reads a lot, but no common sense. Last time I went to buy vegetables, I saw her buying a big-head carp for fifteen yuan a pound!

A: Fifteen yuan! She didn't even haggle? You don't get by like that.

B: She had a super-expensive designer bag, and had powdered her face. Someone like that doesn't bargain.

The woman was both indignant and envious.

A: You're right, she loves dolling herself up. Now that you bring it up, I think she has a lover on the side!

B: Really?

A: I think I've seen him, tall and thin, often comes around during the daytime. You know, that might be the reason that her husband's beating her!

B: What a shameless woman! She deserves it—he should beat her to death! Do you think it's true, though?

A: Yeah! Mrs. Huang suspects it, too.

The two women exchanged a look, both letting out a scornful "hmph!"

Mrs. HE had overheard it all, and was furious, but more than that, she was frightened.

She could rely on nobody.

5

She decided to go to the police.

Two officers were chatting on the street, leaning against their patrol car.

She sobbed as she told them about the details of the abuse, her voice growing weaker and weaker.

Because she knew from their relaxed posture and amused

look that they didn't intend to help her.

She started from the top: "My husband's been beating me, I need the law's help."

The officers exchanged looks, and their attitudes became even more taunting: "The law can't help you."

HE: Why? Am I not a citizen?

One of the officers gave her a playful salute. "The law doesn't protect citizens like you."

6

Suddenly she heard a scream from a nearby alleyway.

There was a tall, dark shadow, holding a big knife, approaching a girl and pulling her to the ground by her hair.

Mrs. HE gulped a breath of cold air: "My God...."

She grasped the office's hand: "Over there!"

The officer looked over, but continued to lean on the car, unflustered, unmoving.

HE: What are you doing! He's committing a crime! He's... He's...

Her face turned red as she heard the sounds in the alleyway.

The look on the officer's face was one of detached pity.

Mrs. HE took two steps back, feeling something wasn't right.

"This can't be happening...it can't be." Her eyes were full

of tears. "My husband abuses me, nobody feels for me; my mother looks down on me, other women blame me; even the law isn't on my side. You cops won't even stop a crime when it's happening in front of you...This can't be real."

She looked around in the gathering dusk, mumbling. "This surely isn't real..."

7

Beeeeeep...

"CONNECTION LOST DUE TO FAULTY LOGIC."

"SWITCHING TO HOST PERSONALITY."

8

The dust faded slowly, revealing a concrete ceiling.

Two prison guards waved a flashlight, checking his pupils.

A guard joked: "Mrs. HE, do you know where you are?"

"This is..."

As soon as he heard these two words come out, he shut his mouth.

This wasn't "her" voice.

It was a deep, raspy, masculine sound.

Why was "he" a man?

He looked down in fright, to see an orange jumpsuit and manacles.

The guard finished checking his body, and ticked a mark on a form. "You can go back and sleep now."

A cement ceiling, iron bars, coldly smiling guards...He got up to run, but the guard turned around, and shoved him back into the prison chair.

"Don't you want to go back and be Mrs. HE some more, HE Saisheng?"

Hearing the name "HE Saisheng," he trembled.

That's right. He remembered. He wasn't Mrs. HE—that was his wife. He was...He was serving a sentence.

And in the long row of prison chairs before him lay convicts of all kinds.

He recognized the careless driver in the accident; the scary man from the alleyway.

They were deep in sleep, eyes spinning rapidly.

The entire room had the atmosphere of a nightmare.

9

[SYSTEM SELF CHECK]

[CONNECTING TO SECONDARY PERSONALITY]

[SCENE NO: 638]

[23 DECEMBER, 2052. TIME: 08:05 AM]

Mrs. HE had finished busying about, and finally was able to sit down at the dining table. Saisheng had already flipped through today's paper with cigarette in mouth.

Mr. HE: Whoa, the government developed a chip that can implant someone else's sensory inputs and memories in your brain, so you can immerse yourself in what they went through. Something this cool—and they're using it in prisons?

Mrs. HE: Oh?

Mr. HE: Extract the victim's memories, and immerse the perpetrator in them. An eye for an eye, tooth for a tooth.

Mrs. HE didn't approve at all;

Mrs. HE: That was Hammurabi's Code. Eye for an eye, both people just end up with one eye.

Mr. HE: You're a real saint, huh? Long on hair but short on sense. If you ask me, this is how it should be.

10

The Alternate Chip allows a person to be implanted with the sights, sounds, and even memories experienced by another. One can be immersed in another's experience, and it's currently widely employed in the penal system.

Complicated sentencing guidelines are a thing of the past: Extracting the memories of a victim—and implanting them in the perpetrator—is the most extreme form of punishment.

An abuser becomes a victim, experiencing his own abuse.

A reckless driver becomes a traffic fatality, crushed under

his own car.

A rapist becomes an innocent girl, assaulted by himself.

Sometimes a judge will decide an eye for an eye isn't enough, and add to the severity of the sentence, using data to manipulate the surroundings of the convict.

HE Saisheng's sentence had been "Hell."

He went back to his cell, thought about all he'd been through, and sobbed. When he'd been beaten by the man in his wife's memories, he was petrified.

But his sentence had only just begun.

Written on the wall, his time remaining was as long as the years he'd abused his wife.

"My husband abuses me, nobody feels for me: my mother looks down on me, other women blame me; even the law isn't on my side."

This was Hell.

0

Mrs. HE had been abused. She sat in the park, phone in hand, scrolling through the calendar.

The weather was unbelievably good, the grass as green as could be. ▪

AUTHOR'S NOTE

This is a soft sci-fi story about domestic violence and the predicament that the victims face. It also attempts to discuss a question: As society develops, the law may become more lenient. But is there still room for ancient legal principles such as "an eye for an eye" and "punish violence with violence"?

ZHAO ANKANG
赵安康

Zhao Ankang, born on October 22, 1994, is a law graduate from the Henan Police College. Since July 2018, Zhao has been working at the Kaifeng Municipal Ecological Environment Bureau. "The Precious Thing" is his only published story so far.

THE PRECIOUS THING

珍贵之物

He lay on top of the dune, motionless, his camouflage uniform conveniently blending into the sand.

The wind howled past, and the ground was like asphalt in summer, generating an unbearable heat.

But he remained still. Beads of sweat gathered into wriggling streams on his face, only to be totally absorbed by the dry air before they could fall. He used to be an excellent soldier of great determination. Of course, he still was.

He held his breath, and he stared with full attention at the battlefield in front of him, which was almost distorted by the scorching sunlight. Although the area was obscured by the sand every now and then, he had to fix his eyes on it, and kill every enemy as soon as they appeared in his sight.

In a world that swirled only with sand, the bodies of enemies were almost welcome embellishments. He blinked slowly. Two consecutive days of guard duty had overloaded his nerves, and such days seemed likely to continue.

Three days ago, when he left the bunker, headquarters had given him an order that had to be obeyed. With mixed feelings, he looked at the vintage-style telegraph transmitter beside him and cursed in his heart: that damn old thing. This "antique" had countless problems—when he sent messages to headquarters, they were able to receive them; this had already been proven. But he had never received any information back. Still, he could not throw it away, because after all, under the current circumstances, it was his only companion.

He just never thought that he would be in this situation one day—nobody had thought that.

Physically, it was unbearable. These days, even when peeing, he dared not move his eyes from the battlefield. He let out a deep sigh. After all, he was not a machine: he had emotions, and he used to have his own family. The long war had dehumanized him. During the war, he relentlessly killed the enemy soldiers; the enemy women and children, whom he kept alive only due to mercy, would probably kill him once he turned his back. To win, everyone had done unethical things. Although his treatment of enemies was somewhat brutal, it worked. Long-term killing had gradually dulled his conscience.

Subconsciously, he touched the metal thing hanging from his neck and smiled. In his indifferent heart, there were still some tender feelings left. A girl's face was unevenly painted in acrylic on the surface of that metal thing, but with the passage of time, some paint had scraped off and the metal showed through at the corners. Over a hundred years ago, people called this thing a phone case.

"Heh," he smiled, as if mocking himself. "It has been a long time, and my memory is also aging." Maybe that was the reason he smiled.

He was not a natural person, but a new product of this lamentable age—a clone.

The girl on the phone case was a classmate in his grade at police academy. Her charming smile and sweet voice had left a deep impression on him; for such a petite girl, she showed such tenacity. During military training, there were some tasks that even he wanted to quit, but this lovely girl persevered without any complaint. Although her shooting results were bad, on the whole she had excelled much more than he did.

He had gradually fallen in love. Whenever he was close to her, he would feel short of breath, just like there was something heavy on his chest. When he got this beautiful photo of her, he printed it on his phone case. He was the kind of person who always had his mobile phone in hand, so each time he took it out of his pocket, he would see her smile. However, as he was shy and not an eloquent talker, he never confessed his feelings to the girl, just watched her quietly. After graduation, the girl made her own career, and he knew that she'd gotten married and lived a happy life...until one day, when she and her husband were traveling abroad, the world war broke out.

The enemy country did not keep to the international laws, so at the start of the war, everyone from his country who had traveled there were seized as hostages, then killed, including her...Peacetimes were always rare throughout human history. Only in turbulent ages did people know the preciousness of peace. It was funny to think that in history, people could wage wars for various strange reasons: religion, land, resources, and even the smile of a beautiful girl.

The scale of the war had gradually expanded since the beginning, and as other countries joined, the struggle became like a seesaw. As time went on, both sides were short on soldiers. People like him, who had police training, also joined the army to answer the country's call (or just to avenge some woman), and involved themselves in the war. Since he showed outstanding performance in battle, he was received by the president, and his blood samples were preserved.

In the middle of the war, some bastard pushed the launch button on nuclear bombs, and the war was immediately escalated. Nuclear bombs exploded everywhere, just like firecrackers, and the explosions did not stop until the surface environment of the Earth was obliterated. Countless people perished, but neither side won, and this had been his last thought before he died.

He let out a heavy breath and ran his tongue over his chapped lips. Now he was a little short of breath—the sun poured its heat onto the ground without any reservation, and as he had been lying on the hot sand for so long, he felt some symptoms of dehydration. Although there was a water bottle tied to his leg, he dared not make any visible movements. The enemy knew that he was in this area, and perhaps they had already sent soldiers to kill him.

He tried his best to collect a little saliva in his mouth, and swallowed it. He gently moved his left hand to his chest and touched the phone case.

The corners of his mouth curled upward.

When he'd woken up in the bunker, he could hardly believe it. His country had mastered cloning technology before the war, and some low-level clones had already participated in various dangerous tasks during the war. Today, as the cloning technology was much more advanced, it only took four months for an embryo to grow into an adult, and some cloned soldiers even had their own consciousness.

Was he still himself after being cloned? He had been thinking about this for a long time. As a cloned adult, at the moment he woke up, he retained all the memories he had had as a natural person. He could remember the taro cooked by his mother; he could remember the happy moments he spent in internet cafes with his friends; and naturally he could remember her, the charming girl in university...But now he was just a tool that could walk, a machine made to kill.

The enemy also mastered this technology, and this meant that the war would continue. How funny it was! You could never escape it even when you died. Although the enemy soldiers were also clones, as long as he thought that one of them used to be the natural person who'd killed the girl, it was difficult for him to let go of his hatred.

A large number of cloned soldiers had been sent out of the bunker. More than a hundred years had passed, but the damage that the Earth suffered was still too monumental to be healed—the surface had become desolate due to nuclear explosions, and the ecosystem was totally destroyed. However, even under these circumstances, what the survivors thought of wasn't how to make up for the mistakes they had made, how to recover the ecology of the Earth. Instead, they were thinking about how to continue the unfinished war.

Due to a shortage of materials, many clones did not even have clothes. The clones on the ground dared not violate the orders issued by their superiors in the bunker. When the first batch recovered their memories, they were dissatisfied with their superiors and rebelled. Thereafter, all cloned soldiers were implanted with remote-controlled bombs, and had no choice but to fight and kill the enemy. If they were lucky, some were able to take the enemies' equipment and other belongings.

Did any of these new clones doubt what they had been told? At least he did not. In this immoral war, he could be considered as having an outstanding military service record. When the superiors, on behalf of the military, asked him what rewards he wanted, there'd been no expression on his face. His family had disappeared a hundred years ago, and the military would not waste their limited resources to clone them. Therefore, he asked the superiors to replicate his old phone case, so as to remember his futile love.

There was a smell of danger in the air, and he felt a little pressure in his chest. Was he nervous? He smiled sardonically, his breath automatically quickened. He tried to slow it down. Was anyone around? He dared not neglect his own instincts, which had been fine-tuned by the long war. In police academy, he ranked second in the camouflage training program. This meant that without professional equipment, it was difficult for average people to detect him, and at this time, advanced equipment was precisely what both sides lacked.

Three days ago, he, who had survived numerous dangerous situations, had followed orders to visit this area with two comrades as well as a vintage telegraph transmitter. The headquarters commanded them to stick to this area. They had faithfully stood guard for three days, and killed more than a dozen enemies. Although their location had already been exposed, they did not retreat. Those were their orders!

The enemies might continue coming here. As long as the resources stored in their underground base were not used up, cloned soldiers would continuously appear. They were only machines made for the war, and no one would grieve their deaths.

In these three days, apart from killing more than a dozen enemies, they had other gains, but he was not permitted to take possession of the spoils of war. Therefore, through the telegraph transmitter, he sent messages about them to headquarters. This morning, the bunker had sent people here to take those things, including several broken guns, some dry food, and all the clothes he had grabbed. In the end, he managed to leave himself two compressed biscuits, because he had already run out of food.

When he and his two comrades arrived, they had not brought much food. One comrade died the first day, and during the night, he and the other comrade dug out a few rats under cover of the darkness. Those little creatures were tenacious enough to survive a nuclear war; they may be the eventual winners.

Three kilometers away from their position, there was a small pond with dirty water. During peacetime, even animals wouldn't drink from there, but he and his comrade gulped greedily, heedless of the nuclear pollution.

The other comrade died the second day. They had been attacked by seven enemies, who were out to kill. However, as they were better skilled, the enemy did not succeed. All seven attackers were killed, but his comrade was also hit. Although the injuries were not to the vital parts, he had to watch the life of his comrade slip away, because he had neither antibiotics nor any medical instruments. Finally, after the repeated pleadings of his comrade, he had suffocated the poor man with his hands.

He did not find any rats on the second day. So what was there to eat? Headquarters did not end up collecting his comrades' bodies. For one thing, they could use their genes to re-clone them. For another, their bodies appeared to be missing some... parts. The cloned soldier who came to collect spoils said nothing, but just shrugged and left.

The enemy came!

Looking forward, he saw two enemy scouts lying on the ground about a hundred meters away.

He sneered, feeling exhilarated, because that was the spot where he had previously killed dozens. He moved into his current position and looked at the two scouts now.

This time, the enemy soldiers might be more skilled. After all, the enemy had already lost a large number of troops. His heart thumped, and his breath came quicker and quicker.

What was the matter with him today? Why did he feel

so uneasy? He touched his phone case and thought, "Protect me." He gripped his AKM, which had killed dozens of enemies. Although he preferred to use the Steyr rifle, in today's situation, it was lucky for him to have an AKM. This assault rifle was produced by the Soviet Union about a hundred years ago, and it must have been a fine product back then.

He raised the rifle, held his breath, and aimed at the two scouts.

Gunshots sounded. The two enemy scouts struggled a few moments, then lay still.

"Did I get them?" he thought. "Are their scouts so useless?" With the caution he had acquired in police academy, he fired a few more shots at the scouts. Then he coldly switched on the safety, picked up his telegraph transmitter, and carefully crawled backward.

Now, he started envying those dead enemy scouts, because at least they had companionship when they died, but he had already been left alone. His two comrades had died one after the other, while he was still alive. After becoming a clone, he would sometimes wonder: If he had been brave enough to bare his heart and be with her, what would have happened?

If they traveled abroad before the war, they might also have died together. "We ask not to be born on the same day, but to die at the same time"—that was the ideal of a couple.

Or what would have happened if the war had not broken out? Those politicians might not have put their citizens' lives at risk for the sake of their so-called "benefit." Who knew for sure? He used to think that after graduating from the academy, he would stay in the force for a few years to gain some experience, and then try to obtain a certificate and become a teacher. The sudden outbreak of the war had turned him into a soldier instead of a teacher.

How sad it was! He had become an excellent soldier who continuously killed enemies on the battlefield, but after so many battles, what did he get? All he owned now was this injured body, as well as the phone case hanging from his neck. Right now, the AKM he held in his hand, and the telegraph transmitter, whose functions were insufficient, might be more precious than him. The waywardness of human beings had totally destroyed the ecosystem, so there were not many natural resources available now. One of the scouts he just killed wore only a pair of boxers, but they should have brought some useful things with them.

Those two were dead, right? Since he started to retreat, those two soldiers had not made any movement. Death? He sneered. The battle had finished; why was he still so nervous? If he had not been a soldier, he might have died peacefully in the bloody nuclear war and would not have been cloned to continue fighting. Over these one hundred years, how many generations of those natural people hidden in the bunker had lived and died? Those people could have their own children, but people like him could only be cloned and used as cheap weapons. Perhaps if he died in battle, the things on his body would also be taken, including his phone case.

He continued to retreat, without knowing why a person as tenacious as himself could suddenly become so tired of the war...but he was unable to kill himself, because when clones were created, they were programmed to be weapons that could not commit suicide. On that thought, if he committed suicide, would the superiors re-clone him? They might not, because a person with a fragile heart was worthless in battle. At this point in his thoughts, he smiled at himself.

A shot sounded, and the stone beside his leg was blasted away.

Were there other enemies ambushing him? Why hadn't he detected it? Shocked, he quickly rolled over on the ground, and subconsciously trained his gun. He froze. *That* was the reason for his quickened breath, his nervousness, and the heaviness in his chest. *That* was the reason...

He did not shoot. He was already unable to do so. The enemy's second shot hit his chest, and blood gushed out immediately.

At the last moment of his life, he held the phone case tightly.

As the enemy's bullets rained down on him, he died with a smile.

The enemy soldier reloaded her gun with an expressionless face. After making sure there were no snipers around, she came up to his body and silently searched for anything of use.

There was something clutched tightly in the left hand of the corpse. What was it? The enemy soldier tried hard to pry his fingers away, and found that it was a worn phone case. But why was there an image of the girl on it so similar to herself? The enemy soldier was confused. She looked at the corpse and felt there was something familiar about this strong soldier who had killed more than a dozen of her comrades, but she couldn't remember anything beyond that. She did not even know what she was supposed to be remembering. But now there was no time to think, because she needed to continue to search the area and kill every enemy she saw.

All she took was the AKM rifle. The phone case was thrown in the sand. Her personal information had been discovered by chance by the senior figures of the military, who found out that she had been the top student of the police academy in their enemy country. Her camouflaging skill ranked first among her class, and her other skills were also outstanding. So she was cloned.

Originally, she was assigned to another area, but when

the scouts found there was an enemy death squad lurking around this area, she was sent here. She did not disappoint her superiors, because she succeeded in the task that had failed seven people yesterday.

Inside the bunker, two researchers were looking at the information on the monitor with tired expressions on their faces.

"Our cloning technology can already accurately and selectively eliminate clones' memories," the first one said before taking a sip of synthetic coffee and stuffing a biscuit into his mouth—material conditions unimaginable for people on the ground. "The spies said that the enemy mastered this technology earlier than us, and they have already applied it to their soldiers."

The second one yawned, saying, "We should also apply this technology as soon as possible, if only to preserve the combat skills of cloned soldiers, and eliminate useless things. Maybe without the interference of their memories, both their abilities to fight and to survive would be much more improved..."

As he spoke, the second researcher pulled up the data of the system's top-ranked soldier, "Let's start with this guy. His record is currently the best in our zone. His clone was killed by a female enemy solider not long ago. Hey, according to the spies' intelligence and old information in the database, the female enemy soldier used to be his classmate when she was still a natural person. They were both trained at the police academy, and her grades seemed to have been a little higher than his."

"Ha, that's interesting indeed," the first one sneered. "Then let's apply our new technology on him."

He lay on the ground silently with his automatic rifle held in hands. He loaded the gun and readied himself to kill enemies at any time.

Just now, he'd mustered all his skills and finally killed a female enemy soldier. That female soldier had been very skilled, and after he'd shot her, he found that she had a pretty face. But no matter how beautiful she was, it was still insignificant on the battlefield.

He had a vague feeling that he knew this beautiful female soldier...but he could not remember anything. Besides, he was too busy to dwell on this strange feeling. The enemy was skilled and strong. How could he dare let himself be distracted?

"That dead woman should only blame her bad luck in meeting me," he thought indifferently.

At this moment, he suddenly found that a well-disguised enemy was quietly hidden in a place not far from him. The enemy got up and rushed towards him with a high-explosive grenade in her hands. With a glance, he found that this enemy had the same pretty face as that female soldier he'd just killed.

But he had no time to feel surprise. All his muscles instinctively contracted, and he quickly raised his automatic rifle, pushed aside all the distracting thoughts, and decisively pulled the trigger. ■

AUTHOR'S NOTE

I wanted to give a unique birthday gift to the girl I like, so I created this story with her as a character and with some memories of our school days. The photo of that girl is indeed on my own phone case. "The Precious Thing" refers to the phone case held by that cloned soldier. The soldier had lived through countless battles, and the phone case is his only comfort in life. In times of peace, the ordinary details of life are what's cherished; ties of blood and friendship are what gives a person the will to live. But in wartime, people may lose their families, their friends, their humanity, and finally their sense of self, becoming just like mindless clones. Originally, the clones were not intended to have memories. But to add more drama and push the plot forward, I finally let him have the ability to remember. It's mentioned in the story that a war destroyed Earth's ecosystem, and I have been working for an environment bureau since I graduated college, which is an interesting coincidence.

THE PRECIOUS THING
Art by Cai Tao (蔡涛)

ZHU YUE 朱岳

Zhu Yue, a lawyer-turned-writer and editor, was named the "Chinese Jorge Luis Borges" by the publishing house of his 2006 short story collection *The Blindfolded Traveler* (《蒙着眼睛的旅行者》). Though Zhu rejects the moniker, it does speak to his style: short stories composed of surreal, imaginative fantasy. Many of his stories start with an absurd premise, only to unfold in surprisingly plausible and logical fashion. Having also been published in People's Literature magazine (《人民文学》), Zhu represents a breath of fresh air in the otherwise realist-dominated landscape of contemporary Chinese literature.

CHAOS OF FICTION

说部之乱

The whole incident began long ago with the babbling of a baby boy. The first words out of his mouth were not "mom" or "dad," but rather complex fragments, such as "it makes no difference," "all through you," and "ugh, sir," which naturally stunned his parents. They believed that other people had secretly introduced the baby to these words, so they decided to move him to a relatively isolated environment. However, the boy's language proficiency grew of its own volition, seemingly free of any external control. He began to articulate complicated sentences: "The driver gazed at me, sighing and astonished," "I shouted savagely"; "You are certainly out of your mind"; and "I am alone, and they are EVERYONE." The frightened parents took the boy to various specialists, from otolaryngology to neurology, to have him studied inside and out. Without any accompanying symptoms, not a single doctor could find anything wrong with the boy. With modern medical science exhausted, the couple turned to witch doctors, shamans, and priests, who provided all kinds of explanations but still couldn't cure the boy.

After many futile attempts to remedy the situation, the child's father started to record every single word the boy said. He had a vague idea that all these words belonged to an integrated system. He also began to show the record to everyone he knew. Finally, a long-parted friend who came back from overseas saw it and told them the origin—the novel *Notes from the Underground* by Fyodor Dostoyevsky. The friend even fetched an old translation from the library and marked everything the boy said. But the boy was far from being a prodigy—he simply recited these sentences randomly and mechanically without comprehending them.

The story attracted extensive attention when it was exposed. People were baffled by this seemingly supernatural phenomenon. Psychologists, linguists, philosophers, geneticists, and even experts in artificial intelligence participated in the study. Eventually, the only explanation from the scientific standpoint was a "coincidence," which really equaled no explanation at all. The expert opinion was no more than to "continue observation"; implying, "until you are tired and forget all about it."

However, the incident quickly grew beyond the experts' expectations. *Notes from the Underground* recited by a baby boy was just an early sign, much like a mysterious crack on a cup's rim. Soon, people discovered that the boy was not alone, as another odd case surfaced. An old, dying man on a hospital bed recited entire passages from *Wuthering Heights* while half-conscious. His family testified that he rarely read any novels.

It is said that to name an inconceivable thing can somehow suppress its power. Based on this belief, the medical world gave the "disease" a beautiful name: romantism. In the beginning, the term was only used in the professional field, but the phoneme soon intensified, turning it into a household name. People who involuntarily uttered excerpts from literature, victims of romantism, increased in number. Besides reciting sentences, their consciousness was seemingly invaded and occupied by different fictional worlds. The patients would fall into a sleepwalking state. Left unattended, they could still seek out water and food out of instinct. However, they would remain listless and senseless, without ever becoming conscious or self-aware again. The condition spread rapidly and became unstoppable. No one was able to find the cause; therefore, nothing could be done for prevention or treatment. People began to blindly destroy fiction books and fled in all directions. All patients were strictly quarantined. However, none of these efforts were effective. In a matter of a few years, the entire world gradually collapsed.

We obtained all the above information much later from

the newspapers of the time, which inevitably contain elements of imagination. As to how we, Lu De and myself, managed to escape, it was a mystery. Perhaps it was because we were far enough from human civilization at the time, both physically and psychologically.

In the first few years after the disaster hit, we were in an unmanned area of the western region, living a life of seclusion. This was thanks to Lu De, who accidentally discovered a legend in the historical records about the ancient Tuva people. Lu De's discovery was that a black dragon once broke out of the ground to terrorize the Tuvas; even their shamans ran out of tricks to defend against it. At that moment, a wandering monk happened to pass by this wild land. He subdued the black dragon and sealed it underground with a small talisman. The Tuvas all vanished around the fourth century, but the legend aroused Lu De's intense interest.

He believed that the black dragon was in fact petroleum erupting, which indicated a possibly rich oil reserve in the land on which the Tuvas had lived. He urged his friends to investigate, but they all dismissed him as a crackpot—such legends were common in various ancient civilizations and were not concrete proof of anything. However, Lu De was persistent in this theory, even somewhat obsessed. He was the kind of person who was intent on destroying his own idealism with failures, but he could never succeed. The reason I agreed, immediately, with Lu De to venture into the untamed land at the time was down to severe misanthropy induced by a failed relationship. I just wanted to go to a trackless wilderness as soon as possible, and hide.

It was a futile attempt at archeology and discovery—there was only desert. Lu De ended up with nothing, but my wish to be left alone was granted. I thought we were sufficiently prepared, but later our supplies were exhausted and passing caravans disappeared. We almost became savages. Faced with this brutal reality, Lu De had to compromise and agreed to return to civilization, replenish our supplies, and resume the expedition. After experiencing great difficulties inherent in returning to the city, we found it wracked beyond recognition by romantism.

We spent more than a year looking for our family and friends, but they had already fallen into oblivion among the chaotic sea of people. As a matter of fact, along with the confusion of human consciousness, the world appeared to be dislocated as well. In our city, large groups of foreigners with romantism were seen in every corner. Later we realized that it was the result of a great civil disorder and large-scale exoduses around the globe. They poured into the city on a tide of insanity. When the tide receded, they were left stranded like scattered rubbish.

We decided to settle down before considering the next move. We picked a university campus as our temporary base and drove away all the sleepwalking people infected with romantism. We managed to find a generator to restore the power supply to the campus. We stored bottled water, petroleum, gas tanks, medicine, all kinds of food, tobacco, coffee, and even alcohol. We had an old pick-up truck that we could drive around to gather the things we needed. One day, without premeditation, we picked two unkempt girls from the street. After they were tidied up, the two girls looked pale, fragile, and in a daze, with empty eyes and slight frames, almost like a pair of dolls. The only difference was that they still had basic survival instincts and mobility. They could speak, but all they said were inscrutable sentences from unrecognizable books. We took the girls in, and not just because of our lust. Our desires were reduced to sand in the untamed wilderness. Perhaps we were just trying to create illusions of normal life through the presence of women. That was also the day that Lu De went for a drive at sunset and returned late at night with a rifle and two boxes of bullets—who knew from where.

We turned two spacious top-floor offices in the main building into bedrooms and lived there with our respective female partners, like two small families. Just like that, we settled down on the campus. Lu De was up very early everyday, had breakfast, and went to the big school library to "do research." At noon, he would get a bite on the bench outside the library and work until half past five, only resting during the weekend. I was puzzled by his insistence on keeping regular hours. He then explained to me in great detail about his motives. As a matter of fact, his reasons were simple. He believed that our existence had lost all frame of reference. Therefore, saving the human race was the only meaningful thing left to do. Since the disaster originated in books, he believed the solution to be in books—those books stacked in the library. This idealist with infinite energy invited me to work with him, just as we did in the desert. However, I was unmoved by his words. I didn't believe in "meaning." To me, the world is a grand enigma, and we are just subtle branches within it—like the stream deep in an abyss shrouded by thick fog; all we have to do is to flow in silence and roll with the tides.

A short while later, Lu De proposed a plan of salvation to me. His strategy was as follows: put together all the possible sentences that could be said by a normal person in their lifetime; then he would construct a novel using these sentences. When this novel occupied the conscience of a subject, this person would be able to master the language of a normal person. Lu De was looking through books such as *Daily English 900* to find examples. After gathering all possible permutations, he would start on the novel. I had to point out that the plan wouldn't have any real effect, because though the number of sentences a person utters during their lifetime is limited, the permutations are infinite; to put it in another way, a person masters not just sentences, but a core method for generating sentences. Lu De agreed that I was right. Unable to contain his disappointment, he aborted his plan to create an "example sentence novel." After that, he proposed many other plans of salvation, but all failed to stand up to even the most cursory scrutiny. His moods rose and fell dramatically with increasingly long hours spent in the library. He gradually became a stranger to me.

I had chosen an alternative way of life. The assignment I put myself to was "to patrol." Twice every morning and evening, I walked along the quiet boulevard to watch over the entire campus with an Akita dog I'd picked up from the streets for company. After I finished with the patrol, I would spend a little extra time taking a walk on the empty school sports field. Along the racetrack, I walked in circles without thinking about anything. There used to be a well-kept lawn encircled by the racetrack. Now, only a few spots of wild grass were left. Sometimes, I would take my female companions and set them in the stands, letting them enjoy the sunshine. In the afternoon, I loved to spend time in a garden tucked in a corner of the campus. The garden may have belonged to botany or horticulture students. There was also a small glass greenhouse outside, which held a board of withered Chinese peony surrounded by excessively growing wild grass. Creepers covered the walls. Under the evening twilight, the glass room reflected a faint yellow luster. The flowers in the field, though faded and decayed, were still able to display distinctive layers of color. Before the afterglow died, I would start my evening patrol.

I also liked to pick a book or two from a small bookstore close to the library, taking them back to my bedroom and flipping through the pages in bed. I would return them once I'd finished. I never set foot inside the library for a book, as I was terribly afraid of the place. It was the territory of the mad Lu De. From time to time, for some reason, I would imagine the library as a giant aquarium and Lu De as a latent sea monster in one of its deep tanks.

Another pastime was listening to my female companion reciting long passages from different novels, like a radio broadcast, as steady patterns of rain fell at dawn, or as the wild wind roared in the night.

"As the train left the station, Robert tarried at the window of his compartment and took a last unemotional look at the island shrouded in a pale, reddish gray mist, and at the sea, where the violet afterglow of the setting sun floated in distant waves..."

"A camp in the open, a countless number of men, an army, a people, under a cold sky on cold earth, collapsed where once they had stood..."

"The three of us remained silent for a while; blankly standing by the gate, staring at the lawn ran riot and the dry, old pond..."

These words were uttered by my female companion, sounding alien and pleasant. She gazed straight ahead, her expression calm and peaceful; her consciousness seemed to be locked away in a fictional world created by the novels. But how could I be sure that I was free? Perhaps I was in the middle of a fiction as well, revisiting the same paragraph again and again.

I used to be keen on literature. In many cases, I could recognize a novel by just a few sentences. However, I had no idea about the fictions my female companion sang. Most of them were obscure to me; after all, there are too many novels in the world.

Winter replaced summer. Just like that, we spent two years on the school campus. It could be said that I enjoyed the distinctive tranquility of surviving the apocalypse, until one gloomy winter afternoon when Lu De came to me to propose his latest theory.

Lu De was emaciated due to his lengthy stays in the library. His skin had become unhealthily pale. He wore his hair long and his eyes were red. The way he spoke sounded nervously excited. Extensive reading over the two years had greatly enhanced his literary merit, making his theory sound delightful and well-versed.

He asked me to read through "The Chamber of Statues" by Jorge Luis Borges carefully. The story goes that, in Andalucía, there was a strong castle with gates that were always locked. Every new king to the throne would add a new lock to the gate. A usurper later ordered the locks removed against the advice of the court and entered the impenetrable castle. In its first room, there were many metal and wooden carvings of Arabic figures. In its last room on the back wall, an inscription could be found, stating that any intruder would be overtaken by warriors that looked like the statues. Before long, the kingdom was indeed conquered by the Arabs. Borges added a note at the end of the story, stating that it was based on the story told on the 272th night of *A Thousand and One Nights*.

"What's the point?" I asked, unable to put my finger on it. Lu De immediately passed me a copy of the *Outlaws of the Marsh*, asking me to read the first chapter, "Zhang the Diving Teacher Prays to Dispel a Plague, Marshal Hong Releases Demons by Mistake," in which Marshal Hong discovered the Suppression of Demons Hall during his visit to a mountain. A dozen seals crossed and overlapped each other on the gate to the hall. The accompanying abbot explained to him: "A Divine Teacher known as the Royal Master of the Way locked the demons in there in the age of the Tang. Each subsequent Divine Teacher added his own seal, prohibiting any successor from opening the doors. If those demons escaped, it would be awful." Marshal Hong didn't believe the abbot and opened the gate against his advice, releasing the demons inside.

Lu De then passed me a third fiction, *Life: A User's Manual* by French writer Georges Perec. On the 20th page, Perec retold the small story of Borges with a larger background: When every king dies and a new king comes to the throne, he would add a new lock to a gate, resulting in 24 locks, each representing a king.

After I finished reading, Lu De presented his theory. From *A Thousand and One Nights* to *Outlaws of the Marsh*, from Borges to Perec, why did they retell the same story of adding a lock or seal? It was very likely that, by writing the novel, they were performing the action of "adding a lock or seal." They were trying to contain the "demon of fiction." Originally, fiction was printed on paper, and was static, like statues. Without a seal, it would become dynamic, even alive, invading people's minds and running rampant. The breaking of the seal led to the great disaster we were experiencing. In order to save humankind and squash the chaos induced by fiction, one had to carry on the work of the author of *A Thousand and One Nights*, Shi Nai'an, Borges, Perec, and many others like them, to retell the story of adding a lock or seal.

When Lu De presented his strange, absurd theory, I was

already working on refuting him. I reminded him of the fact that Borges had read Shi Nai'an and even wrote an article about him once. As for *A Thousand and One Nights* and the 127th night's story, that could be a made-up pretext. Borges certainly could have made it up. So, the story could very well originate from the *Outlaws of the Marsh*, and all Borges had done was to give it a new look. As to Perec, he was just parodying Borges. Everything could be simply explained. Lu De's idea about the seal was too outrageous and entirely unscientific.

To my surprise, Lu De seemed to have little confidence in his latest theory. All the nervous excitement and passion was bluster. My counter-argument soon diminished his willpower. He fell into silence like a ball of flame suddenly extinguished.

It began to snow that very night and didn't stop until the next morning. I woke up languid and sensitive to the chill; I felt like I had a nasty cold. I took my temperature, which confirmed a low fever. I got some medicine from the classroom-turned-warehouse and lay huddled up in bed, skipping the patrol. At almost noon, I heard a crisp, loud gunshot. I anxiously tilted my head to one side, and heard one gunshot after another from the top of the main building in which we resided. Could it be enemies? I sprang up, throwing off the blanket and rushing out of the room.

On opening the small door to the roof, cold air filled my

nostrils. Large flakes of snow poured down, blurring my sight. But I immediately saw Lu De, laying on his stomach on the snow-covered ground and shooting in the air. It was in the direction of the sports field, already a vast expanse of whiteness.

"Who are you shooting at?" I asked.

"I was shooting at the snowflakes; they are endless," said Lu De.

"Don't freeze yourself," I said.

"I don't care." He sat up and smiled a little at me.

"Come down with me and we'll eat something hot together."

"No, thanks. I want to stay for a while."

"OK."

I returned to my room, somewhat worried. But the gunshots completely died down. It was clear to me that his hopes were only wild, feckless fantasies. When they burst, all that would be revealed would be sharp, unforgiving reef. Right now, Lu De had to learn to live with, even gaze into, this reef.

After taking the cold medicine, I became drowsy and soon fell into deep sleep. The uneasiness turned into disturbing nightmares. At last, I was awoken by a loud noise, unflustered this time. I carefully got dressed and slowly strolled to the roof. The snow had stopped. On the horizon, a corner of a dark cloud lifted, revealing a bright red setting sun. I found Lu De in a pool of blood in a corner. He was already dead. He sat down, pointed the gun to his chin and pulled the trigger.

Later, I attempted to carry on with my old pattern, but every time I passed the now dark library during patrol, I sensed a vague restlessness. The ghost of Lu De seemed to linger inside. I now know that the peaceful illusion I built over the last two years had shattered into pieces with that gunshot. Every time I recalled Lu De's suicide, I always wondered: If a person knows that he has only two or three hours left, would the world, in his eyes, turn into a sort of film or novella?

I tried not to contemplate the fact that "I was the only person left with consciousness," but I could no longer live an easy life. I considered the idea of moving away from the campus, to look for a wild, primitive beach to build a small cabin and reconstruct the peaceful illusion. However, I felt that I had to complete a mission before I left; otherwise, Lu De's spirit would keep haunting me. This was a subtle sense of responsibility. So I took in Lu De's last theory, and have started to write a story of "adding a lock or seal." I will run away as soon as it is complete. At this moment, the beach in waiting flicks in front of my eyes—the musky tide slaps against the bare reef, roaring to remind me to gaze into it. ■

AUTHOR'S NOTE

I came up with this story when I was working as an editor in a publishing company. Immersed in fiction every day, I would end up reading lengthy novels like *Look Homeward, Angel* by Thomas Wolfe three or four times. My mind seemed to be somewhat eroded by them. The atmosphere in my office was cold and indifferent, and I rarely talked to my co-workers. I only knew that they were also reading all kinds of novels. Such depression led to despair, but I found a plus side to the despair; it gives you a clear head, as it is what's left after the illusions of life shatter. However, it was also hard to endure. This is probably the inspiration for "Chaos of Fiction." In addition, the similarities between certain plots, such as the adding of a seal in *Outlaws of the Marsh* and the story about the locked gate told by Jorge Luis Borges, gave me inspiration for the story.